To f.

Happy reading

C000225533

L Loveday

Kate Lily Loveley is the pen name of the author, who felt compelled to use the names of her female ancestors, as a unique way of keeping their memory alive.

Kate Loveley was the birth name of her maternal great grandmother. Lily, the Christian name of her paternal Grandmother. Alice, the title and main protagonist, was her maternal grandmother.

Her love of writing began with a gift of a five year lock up diary at the age of seven and she has never stopped writing since.

To my family with love.

To the reader, I hope you enjoy
reading this story of Alice.

KL Loveley .

Katie Lily Loveley

ALICE

AUSTIN MACAULEY
PUBLISHERS LTD.

Copyright © Katie Lily Loveley (2017)

The right of Katie Lily Loveley to be identified as author of this work has been asserted by her in accordance with section 77 and 78 of the Copyright, Designs and Patents Act 1988.

All rights reserved. No part of this publication may be reproduced, stored in a retrieval system, or transmitted in any form or by any means, electronic, mechanical, photocopying, recording, or otherwise, without the prior permission of the publishers.

Any person who commits any unauthorized act in relation to this publication may be liable to criminal prosecution and civil claims for damages.

A CIP catalogue record for this title is available from the British Library.

This book is a work of fiction based on my own observations. The names, characters, places, organisations and incidents are products and exaggerations of the author's imagination. Any resemblance to actual events, persons living or dead is entirely coincidental.

ISBN 9781786129727 (Paperback)
ISBN 9781786129734 (Hardback)
ISBN 9781786129741 (E-Book)

www.austinmacauley.com

First Published (2017)
Austin Macauley Publishers Ltd.
25 Canada Square
Canary Wharf
London
E14 5LQ

My sincere thanks to my husband Michael, for his patience throughout the many long hours I abandoned him to his own space, while I was totally absorbed with writing *Alice*.

To my clever and talented daughter, Annalisa, for her unfailing encouragement and support.

To my son. Nathan who came on board when it mattered, by providing professional and commercial support, getting *Alice* to publication.

To Graham, Kevin and Jennifer, for making my family complete.

Finally, to Austin Macauley Publishers, for believing in my novel, giving me the opportunity to fulfil a lifelong ambition.

INTRODUCTION

Fate draws together the lives of Alice and Robin. The trials and tribulations of divorce, followed by the struggles of becoming a step parent, takes its toll on Alice, who escapes the over whelming tensions by turning to alcohol, resulting in the deterioration of her health and wellbeing. The story follows the process of the positive sunny nature of Alice, being chipped away until she feels all is lost. At the lowest point in her life, she decides that above all else she will become the heroine of her own life. Not the victim.

CHAPTER ONE

A ray of light found its way through the fraction of a gap in the badly closed bedroom curtains; this was enough stimulation to rouse Alice from yet another night of restless sleep. She could feel the light penetrating her tightly closed eyelids, beckoning Alice to open her tired bloodshot eyes. She was in the twilight zone, between sleep and waking, her mind still charged with the emotions of the traumatic dreams which consumed her restless over-active mind. Her eyelids appeared to be the only part of her body she could consciously connect with, and the sheer effort of opening them was paramount to a movement against the force of gravitational pull as the first spectrum of light penetrated the tiny slit of exposed cornea between upper and lower lids. Alice not only felt the ache behind her eyes, but also the deep rooted pain from the tight muscle fibres, across her shoulders, radiating down bilateral sides of her neck, burning deep into the tissues and exciting the nerves into spasm.

A quiet groan escaped from her parched lips as Alice gingerly propped herself up in bed, gently resting her head and shoulders against the supporting pillows. She looked at the clock on her bedside table. It was seven fifteen, much too early to be rising on a Sunday morning. Alice swung her legs over the edge of the mattress, trying not to disturb her husband Robin, who was sleeping soundly beside her. He looked so peaceful and settled, not a care in the world, thought Alice, he was stretched out with his feet hanging out of the bed, no doubt to cool them down from the heat of the duvet.

Making her way to the bathroom as quietly as possible, she closed the bathroom door. A light breeze was blowing the window blind, sucking the blind backwards and forwards towards the open window. Alice shuddered. The sound of the toilet flushing disturbed Robin from his sleep. He called out to his wife, enquiring if she was okay. He was well aware of her restless sleep, for unknown to Alice, her constant tossing and turning disturbed him also, although he was fortunate enough to slip back into sleep quite easily.

Robin knew the source of his wife's tension and how she struggled to cope with the daily family dramas and the increasing responsibility she endured at work. Robin understood how difficult life had become at home. Indeed, he was well aware of the difficulties and trials and tribulations that Alice endured with his family. He had witnessed this first hand and was well aware how much worse the situation was for Alice when he was not around. Lately, he too, had felt the rising tensions in the family home and was frustrated because he knew that sooner or later, Alice would approach him to try and initiate a serious discussion about their present predicament and their future. Predictably of course he would try and avoid the situation using any excuse he could muster. Robin had tried this approach with her many times in the past, but Alice could be like a dog with bone; sometimes she would not let go. He also knew her to be a woman of her word and if she made a promise or commitment, she felt duty bound to undertake her obligation and would let nothing stand in her way. He hoped she felt the same determination with respect to her wedding vows no matter how much she was put to the test. He consciously tried his best to help make the situation less difficult for his wife, but in doing so he often overcompensated for his children who possessed no sense of teamwork and took full advantage of the lifestyle he and Alice provided. But today was Sunday, he and Alice had worked hard all week and he wanted to show her just how much he loved her.

"I'll bring you a mug of tea then have a nice soothing shower," said Alice as she slipped on a soft towelled bath robe and her mules which she had purchased during a spa hotel holiday they had enjoyed in Turkey two years previous. Robin watched Alice as she climbed out of bed, wearing her black satin camisole with tiny shoe string straps. He admired her petite body and her long tousled hair which this morning was shining and healthy. Her femininity was so appealing. He thought back to the time when they first met, ten years ago. Alice was just getting over the traumatic divorce from her first husband, after twenty-two years of marriage. It had been a difficult time for her, discovering the infidelity and betrayal of a husband she had trusted and loved. Because of this trauma, Alice had lost a lot of weight and was only seven stone when they met and, although in proportion, he was worried that if she took ill, there was no weight on her to sustain her and keep her strong. Robin had lost his first wife to leukaemia and was well aware of the need to keep healthy and strong. Around the time of Alice's discovery of her husband's affair and the end of her marriage, Robin's life had been thrown into pain and despair with months of worry and sadness, finally leaving him with the loss of his beloved wife and the mother of his four children, Gary, Wayne, Stephen and Julie.

Alice had helped Robin come to terms with his loss while trying to overcome her own emotional roller-coaster.

Alice had found it difficult at first, to trust another man, but with the help of her friends she had gradually grown accustomed to the dating game which was new territory for her. She had been sixteen when she met her first husband and although she had previous adolescent relationships, they had mostly been with old school friends whom she had felt safe and comfortable with. In any case, more often than not she had usually socialized in groups. Alice had been courting her first husband five years when they married. It was the accepted progression of relationships in the early 1970s.

Courtship, engagement then marriage before the age of twenty-five. Alice was only a few weeks from her twenty first birthday when she married. Most of her friends were already married with children. It was considered a worry to young women in her village not to be married by the age of twenty-five. However, having a family was another matter. They waited five years before deciding to become parents. Mathew was born into a well prepared loving family and three years later he had a sister, Anne Marie, making their family complete.

Years later when Alice looked back at the pictures of herself post marriage break up and compared them to the happy family photographs with her children. She saw a frail, sad looking creature, caught on the camera as opposed to the happy family pictures of the many holidays and special occasions they had shared together. It was in this post traumatic period of her life when Alice ventured out into the unknown territory of singleton.

The very first time she went out with her friends was to a well-known local singles bar.

Alice felt uncomfortable the moment she entered the smoke filled room. Her first impression was to liken the venue to a cattle market full of many cows and a disturbingly equal number of bulls. The cows were dressed up like male peacocks strumming around with their full plumage on display. Everyone stood shoulder to shoulder already making body contact with whoever happened to be standing either side, men waved £20 notes in the air trying to catch the attention of the obviously overworked bar staff, shouting their drinks orders above the noise of the crowd and the music.

The one and only saving grace of the night for Alice was the music as the gravelled voice of Rod Stewart singing "Maggie May" rang out above the buzz of the crowd. Alice wondered how she was going to squeeze in amongst this circus, but somehow along with her friends she did, and half an hour later, she was stood pressed against a wall with a large glass of red wine in her hand, holding on to it tightly for fear of being elbowed and spilling it down herself, or even worse, one of her friends. Not used to flirting and chatting to strange men that first experience as a new forty something single had been hellish for her. My god, thought Alice, is this going to be my life from now on? Standing in a cattle market being looked up and down like a prized Heifer? The thought had kept her awake for many a night, reinforced by the knowledge that her now ex-husband was sleeping soundly with the new woman in his life who he had chosen over herself, and she surrendered to the fate of an uncertain future.

Her friends, of course, had observed Alice's distress and how she had stood uncomfortably first on one foot then the other, fidgeting all night like a virgin in a brothel. The following week her friend Kay organised a girls' night in, which turned out to be an evening of enlightenment for Alice as they each discussed their own personal problems and fears they had encountered on their own early step into singleton.

Apparently, Alice had been giving off the wrong signals with her body language and demeanour which could be interpreted as "don't come near me. I'm not available". Alice explained she didn't feel available. What she had felt was vulnerability for any gold digging lothario who might fancy their chance. Her friends tried to reassure Alice that she wouldn't always feel that way and perhaps next time they all went out together, she may take on board what they had said. Relax a little more and enjoy the evening.

It was good to be in the company of her friends, but soon it was time to wish them all goodnight and head off home. That night as she tossed and turned in bed; all she could think about was the pain of betrayal which was striking deep into her heart like a physical blow. She tried to close her eyes, but sleep eluded her. A million thoughts turned round and round in her head, a mix of emotions tumbled around in the pit of her stomach, anger, pain and abandonment. Alice knew she needed a good dose of self-confidence to lift her back up so she could begin the next chapter of her life. She was aware that she could be considered by some as a good catch. She owned her own home, had a very good job with a comfortable pension and her own car. She was aware that she was a little underweight but could still look good in the right clothes.

Disapproving of her brother's behaviour, her sister in law had arranged a day of pampering shortly after her brother had moved out of the family home. Alice's long hair was in a terrible unhealthy condition and had been falling out due to the stress of her marriage break up. She looked like an extra in the lion king with an unruly mane.

It was a rash decision, but at the time nothing really mattered except her two children and getting through the next day, so she had her hair cut off and shaped into a very short spiky style which was apparently fashionable, something which Alice had totally lost touch with. The first time she saw her reflection, Alice was horrified, her thin stressed face, framed by a short crop of dull, lifeless hair, reminded her of the lovely ladies she had met at the hospice who were on chemotherapy. Her heart sank deeper and deeper. Observing her mum's low mood. Anne Marie decided to help her mum to choose some new outfits to match this short, trendy elfin like mum. So one Saturday morning they caught the train to London. The two-hour train journey was a nice break from driving. Anne Marie was wonderful company and Alice loved her dearly, so very soon she was relaxed and enjoying herself. When they arrived in London it was raining, but nothing was going to spoil this day as mother and daughter made their way to Oxford Street with one mission in mind: to create a new look for Alice. Anne Marie tried to steer her mum away from the slightly bohemian style clothes that she generally chose, which, although suited her and gave Alice the appearance of a mother, was not the image needed to begin the next journey of her life. Eventually, with a lot of help from her daughter, Alice agreed to purchase a collection of trendy but sophisticated items.

She purchased a variety of silk blouses and shirts, stylish cashmere sweaters and fine lacy underwear. Instead of the usual ankle length flowing skirts she chose a variety of well-tailored pencil skirts and court shoes with seductive kitten heels. Anne Marie suggested her mum would need a few accessories instead of her usual long beads and coloured bracelets, so off they went to search out the markets. First stop was at Camden Lock market which was buzzing with locals and tourists, then they went to Notting Hill and finally back to Oxford Street. Exhausted, they finally sat down to eat before catching the tube from Oxford Circus back to St Pancras. They boarded the train happy and exhilarated from a wonderful day in the city. Alice went home with a warm feeling of hope enveloping her whole body like a comfort blanket, Anne Marie was satisfied her truly wonderful mum had made the transition she needed and was proud of herself for being the catalyst in this transformation.

With her new look and a few tips from her friends, it wasn't long before she was being wined and dined by a number of would-be suitors. This, of course, boosted her confidence, which had taken a battering when her husband had swapped her for a younger model. Alice enjoyed the attention and like a flower she began to blossom. When before she had felt like a flower trapped by weeds, strangled and choked, now she stood proud and radiant. Alice began to gain weight, she learned how to arrange her hair so that it flattered her fine elfin features, and she began to apply little make up and a new fragrance. No longer the wallflower, she was developing into a strong, confident woman once more.

Already well educated and a registered nurse, Alice decided to further her education. She had studied for a qualification in science and literature after qualifying as a nurse and always enjoyed studying, so she decided to enrol on an Open University degree course to study biological science.

Always interested in a variety of scientific subjects, she began her foundation year by choosing physics, chemistry, biology and earth science. This involved a lot of dedicated study time, leaving no room to feel sorry for herself. Looking after Mathew and Anne Marie, working full-time and studying for a degree soon filled every moment of her life. Once a month she went to the local university, met other students and attended lectures. What a wonderful week of summer school that had been in her first year of study

Meeting new friends, attending fascinating lectures with hands on experience in the laboratories left Alice with a thirst for knowledge which was to remain with her forever.

The days in the classroom were long, the evening lectures tiring, but the late night socializing was a revelation for Alice. Her first week of many she would spend at summer school was a tremendous success and most enjoyable. Her children constantly encouraged their mum with her studies and were both so proud. Four years later, along with Robin and Alice's mum, they watched Alice climb the stage at the Harrogate International Centre to accept her BSc in biological science. Throughout the first year of her studies, her divorce had been proceeding.

Alice knew it was in motion and had accepted the outcome as inevitable, so was well prepared when the divorce absolute came through.

Having experienced the single life for a year, Alice wondered if she preferred this easy, uncomplicated lifestyle. Although she enjoyed the attention of a few of the men who could be considered suitable for a long term relationship, none of them truly appealed to her and the idea of becoming intimate on any level filled Alice with fear. She had only been intimate with one man and he had betrayed her. Alice wondered if she would ever be ready to give herself to another man. That was until she met Robin. They had met briefly in the past. His first wife had worked as a physiotherapist at the hospital and on occasions, as couples, they had enjoyed meals out together, during which the men had the usual male conversations around sport and politics and the women chatted about their children and the latest hospital gossip. Therefore, having previously met, their first encounter was as old acquaintances catching up on each other's lives and discussing family.

Over many months their friendship blossomed into love and a remarkable thing happened to Alice. She finally learned to trust another man. Eventually, six years after her marriage had ended, she was ready to be a wife once more. Despite the battering her trust had taken, Alice never lost faith in the idea of love. She had considered herself to be happily married once, and she was not disillusioned with men; just the one that had mattered to her.

Robin watched his wife and a little smile of satisfaction lightened his face. Although still petite and practically perfect, she had managed to gain the two stone in weight he had encouraged when they first met. Robin had never hidden the fact from Alice that he would like her to gain a few pounds. When Alice had asked what he had seen in her if he desired her to be a size larger, Robin answered that he had seen potential.

This did not necessarily convince her. Sometimes she wondered if he preferred her to resemble his first wife, who was three dress sizes larger than herself. Despite this, she had managed to gradually increase her weight over time and while her friends were all desperately trying to shed a few pounds Alice had been able to enjoy the freedom of choice at meal times. Contentment within her marriage in the early years had increased her appetite, aiding Alice with her quest.

As Alice left the bedroom, she heard Robin switch on the television with the remote control. She knew he would be watching the news channel to catch up on current affairs and as he so often joked, "I have to watch the news, we might be at war." Alice laughed at this, but recently she felt she was already at war within herself, struggling to make a very important decision. Alice stepped carefully off the last step of the stairs. The hallway floor had been removed and a temporary walkway installed by the builders leading into the downstairs cloakroom and the kitchen. She breathed a deep sigh, still feeling the distress from the flood damage that had occurred six months previously following weeks of heavy rain in most regions of England. Some areas had suffered extreme flooding with rivers bursting their banks, resulting in utter chaos with extreme property damage and many families were left homeless. The extent of the damage to their own home was a result of the soak away drainage system located beneath the front lawn being unable to cope with the torrents of rain which had run from the guttering. The house had been extensively extended by the prior owners, but despite the increased surface area of the roof and guttering, the soak away had not been enlarged to take the extra volume of water. The combination of the extreme weather and inadequate drainage had resulted in a breach of the damp proof layer of the property. It was the extension on the house which had appealed to them from the very first moment they had spotted the house. It had been sheer luck they had found the house, after many months of searching for a suitable location and a house large enough to accommodate themselves, Robin's four grown up children and Alice's son. Her daughter Anne Marie had no plans to live with her mum and stepfather as she was working in the city and renting a shared house with friends. However, a room would need to be available should her circumstances change.

The morning they discovered the house it was love at first sight, even before they viewed the property their gut feelings felt positive. Alice was so certain this was the place for them she couldn't wait to visit the estate agent to arrange an appointment to view the property, but instead Alice promptly rang the doorbell and made direct enquiries with the home owner. The owner invited Robin and Alice to view their home there and then. With open minds they inspected the house. The house fulfilled all of their requirements. It had six bedrooms, a large kitchen, large utility room, a dining room, an L-shaped lounge, large bathroom, one en-suite bathroom and a downstairs cloakroom. The icing on the cake was a conservatory opening onto a private garden which was laid to lawn with established borders and a bank of conifers providing perfect privacy.

They both agreed this was exactly what they had been looking for. The house layout could have been designed with their own needs in mind. The location, a quiet cul-de-sac on a small development was most suitable to their needs. The driveway would easily accommodate four cars and with their family this would be essential.

Luck was with them; Alice sold her home within a week of Robin selling his. The capital from both homes enabled them to buy the house for cash, leaving them mortgage free. Their new home was available for them to move into on the same day as both the contracts on their individual homes were exchanged. Their wedding was held two weeks before the house sale. A one week honeymoon in Italy was arranged two days following their wedding, which enabled their respective children to remain in their own homes for one final week and for themselves to be around for the final packing and the big move.

A well-organized person, Alice had more or less packed everything ready for transferring into the removal van, with the exception of the large pieces of furniture and the white goods. Her large refectory table she herself dismantled, the chests and bedside cabinets were all dismantled and taped together. Her possessions were neatly boxed and labelled and the majority of the curtains and blinds had been taken down, washed and neatly folded away. Alice was well prepared. Unfortunately, neither Robin nor his family had made any attempt to prepare for the big move, despite Alice desperately trying to encourage Robin and his children to carefully pack and label their personal possessions.

On the day of the move from Robin's house it was total disaster and chaos. Robin and his family tipped everything out of their drawers and cabinets directly into large black plastic sacks. Kitchen and bathroom objects were pushed into cardboard boxes with no care for the fragility of some items. A friend of one of the boys appeared with a trailer on the back of his car and this was used to take away broken and unwanted furniture to the local council dump. A number of visits to the dump were made, following removal of further items from the garage and loft. One by one the rooms were emptied until Alice could finally enter the house to clean through ready for the next occupant.

Despite Alice's own carefully made plans to have a smooth transition from one home to the next, it had not materialised. The contracts were officially exchanged at six pm on a Friday, and all parties agreed to move on the Saturday morning. With this in mind, Alice had booked a removal van for early Saturday morning. However, the young first time buyer of her property was so eager, that at five o'clock on the Friday, he telephoned Alice at home, who wasn't in, but Mathew was. He left a message saying that it was his house after six pm and he was moving in that evening. Mathew promptly rang his mum at work, resulting in Alice leaving early and frantically contacting the van hire company and arranging a van for Friday evening as well as Saturday morning in anticipation of storing her belongings overnight in a removal van. She rang Robin and some of her friends, who all rallied round and moved her whole home into a van, just as the new owner turned up with his own furniture van. The only saving grace of the whole event was the good fortune that the house Alice and Robin were buying had been emptied that afternoon so Robin collected the key Friday evening instead of Saturday morning. It was- past midnight when they emptied the van of furniture, white goods and the many packing boxes and suitcases. Robin and Alice went to bed exhausted knowing they had to empty Robin's house the next day. Between them they had five sofas, two washing machines, three fridges, two freezers, three double beds, four single beds, a number of chests, wardrobes, cabinets, tables, chairs and household goods. There were bikes, lawnmowers, garden tools and sundries, box upon box of kitchen equipment ornaments. Lamps and books, numerous bags of towels, bedding, curtains and clothes. The list had been endless.

Finally they had moved into the house which was to become their dream family home.

A home where they could build on their marriage and forge good relationships with extended family.

Indeed, the house lived up to their very expectations. That was, until the day the rain water had started to seep under the foundations of the house, seeping into the floors and rising up the walls, ruining the plaster and the floors of their beautiful home. Their hallway and downstairs cloakroom were damaged from the rising water resulting in the supporting joists and battens becoming severely damaged. Thankfully the kitchen had been spared from damage, which was a blessing. The kitchen was Alice's pride and joy. It had cost all of her savings, which she felt was worth the expense as it made up the difference of investment she had made when they purchased the house.

This was an important issue for her in the long term as she wanted to be recognised as having equal share in the house.

Between them, Robin and herself had carefully planned the design of the kitchen employing a project manager and a reliable company to install. They chose solid French oak wood, which was in a natural state with the knots of the wood visible, giving a rustic country look which was reinforced by the addition of pewter handles, an authentic range cooker and the electrical appliances integrated behind the oak panel doors.

The pièce de résistance, her favourite piece of furniture, was the large dresser which stood in the dining area of the large kitchen. The dresser, with its two glass cabinets and open shelves, was where Alice displayed her prized collection of antique tureens, jugs and plates. In the illuminated glass cabinets she displayed her collection of fine crystal-ware, most of which were wedding gifts from family, and the exquisite champagne flutes herself and Robin had purchased during a memorable holiday with their friends when they visited Prague for a long weekend. Alice just adored collecting antique objects, she had a special interest in ceramics and occasionally Robin and herself would visit a local auction house and bid for something special. Robin was also interested in collectables. He particularly had an interest in clocks; with an ambition to one day own a grandfather clock. Robin already had a place marked out in the lounge he deemed suitable. They already owned a Westminster chime mantel clock that Robin had purchased from a local antiques fair which stood pride of place on an oak mantel table in the lounge. Their home was a good mix of old and new that blended together well, giving an eclectic feel to the home.

Alice entered the kitchen looking around with a deep feeling of satisfaction. She loved this room. The wintry sun shone through the kitchen window reflecting on the pine kitchen table and chairs, which had been strategically placed there to allow for the penetration of maximum light during the winter months and the bright sunshine in summer, thus giving a welcome feel to the dining area.

The large bowl of fruit in the centre of the table was piled high with fresh fruit which Robin had kindly purchased on his way home from work on Friday. Robin always took on the mammoth task of the family shop, which, with six adults to provide food and drink for, was an extremely expensive shopping bill. It was one of the many bones of contention building up and festering inside Alice, eating away, waiting to erupt any day now.

She glanced at the fruit bowl, making a mental note to use some of the apples in the red cabbage dish she was planning to serve with the roast turkey and accompaniments around half past two when they would be joined by her mum and Robin's dad. The sweet and sour red cabbage dish was one of her favourite vegetable dishes to compliment white meat and pork. Her first mother in law was of German origin and had taught her to cook some traditional German dishes. Alice herself had lived in Germany for a number of years which had been an interesting and most enjoyable experience, one which she truly appreciated, as having the opportunity to live in a different country was an experience that she felt had enhanced her life.

Sometimes Alice would reflect on her years spent in the black forest in Bavaria. She was young then and a new bride with so many hopes and inspirations. A smile forced its way into her face as she remembered her first few weeks in the village. Having a limited knowledge of the language, they ate only pork chops and potatoes for the first week as she had purchased far too many of each. The conversion to metric values was something she had needed to learn along with an improved knowledge of the language. That first bag of potatoes she had carried home from the small grocery shop had been huge and extremely heavy. The grocer must have thought she was quite insane, reflected Alice.

Even now, each Christmas, she prepared a traditional German plate full to the brim with fruit, nuts, biscuits, gingerbreads and chocolates. And she felt that some traditions should be passed on. Alice hoped the Christmas plate would remain as part of her future grandchildren's traditional Christmas.

She filled the kettle while gazing through the kitchen window, which overlooked the back garden. Alice never tired of admiring the view from this window. Throughout the changing seasons the garden mesmerised her. The resilience of nature as the first snowdrops pushed up through the hard permafrost of the land; the beauty of spring when colour burst into the garden as the many daffodils, tulips and narcissi – which she planted the first autumn after they had bought the house – nodded their heads in the early spring breeze. During the summer months the garden continued to be a blaze of colour from the array of petunia, lobelia, marigold and nasturtium which Alice lovingly planted in the borders. There was an abundance of urns and tubs scattered around the patio area, which they had laid with paving stones imported from India. In these she planted red, white and pink geraniums, reminding her of faraway Mediterranean holidays which she had shared with her family and with Robin.

Now as she earnestly looked out of the window there was a light scattering of frost and a ray of weak winter sunlight creeping through the clouds, adding a glisten to the tiny drops of water on the stone bird table that her parents had made for her fortieth birthday. She breathed a deep sigh, remembering the two other gardens the bird table had enhanced. For three years it had stood majestically in the small back garden of the house she had shared with her first husband. The house where her children were born, the little garden where they had played as children. The garden had also been home to

29

Anne Marie's pet rabbit Snuggles. What a good life Snuggles had, thought Alice. She was allowed to freely roam the garden from dawn to dusk, going into her cosy hutch every evening, following a simple prompt from Anne Marie. Consequently, Snuggles lived to a ripe old age. A little smile crept over Alice's face as she remembered the mounds of rabbit mess she regularly swept from the patio area.

Following the divorce, Alice was intent on saving enough money to move up the property ladder and into a detached house, which she eventually achieved by working in her full time position in addition to working as a supply nurse to provide weekend hospital cover. The bird table went with her, providing a free lift to a perky little frog which had sat in the bowl and much to Alice's surprise jumped out at her as the table was lifted out of the removal van. However, within a year of achieving her ambition, Alice was on the move again, this time with Robin and into their first home together. Consequently, once again the table went with her, but minus the frog that time. Her love of gardening she had inherited from her father, who kept an allotment in addition to the small garden that surrounded their family home. There was always a supply of fresh vegetables and soft fruits such as blackcurrants, strawberries and gooseberries to be shared amongst the family.

When Ann Marie was a small child she loved to spend time with her granddaddy in the allotment and as she grew up her love of the land had continued. Both Alice and her brother were keen gardeners, a very useful interest to have inherited.

Looking out of the window, her attention was drawn to the garden swing, as a light breeze set it gently rocking. It was covered in debris from the conifers and would need a good clean before the summer arrived. She looked up towards the conifers, hoping to catch sight of the other robin in her life; the little bird with its proud red chest and friendly attitude. That morning, there was no sign of her favourite little bird. Perhaps she might see him later, while she drank her mid-morning coffee in the conservatory that backed onto the garden, giving tremendous views and a very useful place to store her more tender plants away from the winter frosts.

There was a time when she had hoped to have a greenhouse, but perhaps now wasn't the time to be dreaming of such additions to the garden. Staring out of the window, Alice was lost with her thoughts, troubled by what she knew she must discuss with her husband. The sooner she did, the sooner the heavy burden of stress hopefully would begin to ease and release the tension she felt throughout her body. Her troubling thoughts were overridden by the sound of a click from the kettle, signalling the water was boiled. If only my problems would evaporate into the air like the steam from the kettle, thought Alice as she made herself a coffee. The lovely aroma as the hot water hit the granules relaxed her a little, allowing Alice to concentrate on the task in hand.

Robin preferred tea in the morning, so while the tea was brewing Alice sipped the freshly made coffee. The best drink of the day was always the very first one following a restless night's sleep.

Alice carefully carried the mugs up the stairs, each one balanced on a saucer, which always amused Robin. He said she was the only woman he knew who was so fastidious as to use a saucer with a mug. Just one of the many things which made Alice different. And Robin and Alice were certainly different from each other in many ways. Fundamentally, they had different views and opinions. Alice tended to have a positive outlook in life, always looking for the good in a person or situation.

Mathew, on a number of occasions, said his mum would have made a good defence lawyer and would probably have found something good to say about the Kray twins. Robin tended to be more negative and pessimistic, and probably more realistic than his wife. Very apt with quips, Robin could also be unashamedly sarcastic which Alice found difficult to cope with at times.

While Alice enjoyed continued learning and trying new activities, Robin was content to watch the television or go to the local pub. He preferred going to working men's clubs where he could enjoy a game of bingo and watch live entertainment. Of course, Alice joined her husband on these occasions, enjoying the entertainment herself but not the bingo or the meat raffles, which she found most amusing when the prize of a pack of sausages was won.

Robin knew his wife well, having observed the many different challenges she set herself, some of which were still ongoing, like attempting to learn to play the acoustic guitar, which Anne Marie's fiancé had kindly given to her along with some books and a guitar tuner. Not naturally gifted in this area and probably tone deaf, Alice admitted this was quite challenging for her. However, having attended a six month foundation course in Spanish at the local college she was improving her Spanish language skills, which she achieved by utilizing her time efficiently while ironing. While Alice smoothed away the creases, she listened to her Spanish tapes and babbled away quite happily to herself, much to the amusement of the rest of the household.

Never standing in the way of her new pursuits, Robin stood by as Alice attempted to learn tap and ballet and readily agreed when she suggested they try salsa dancing together. They were both rubbish, of course, neither of them could wriggle their hips or look remotely comfortable on the dance floor. Alice said it didn't help that Robin, being left handed, led by the left and they could only attend on alternate weeks because of Robin's shift pattern. Consequently, they missed half of the set program of moves and were always behind the rest of the class. They did have many weeks of fun, eventually giving it up as a lost cause.

Alice was always busy on one level or another. When her mood was low she wrote poetry, some of which she would read to Robin who pretended to be interested, but in truth wasn't in the least bit paying attention. Reading books of historical and modern romance was also a favourite pastime for Alice, especially when away on holiday. She had always been an avid reader, having read the classics many times in addition to going to the theatre to watch productions of some of the popular classics. Interested in health and fitness over the years she had attended a number of fitness classes such as Pilates, yoga and aerobics.

When Anne Marie had the time they would occasionally play badminton together. Alice had hoped to persuade Robin to play badminton with her, she knew he had played well when he was in his thirties, but he declined as he was concerned his knees might get painful with the force of resistance when running. She also tried to persuade him to go swimming with her and to be fair he did go on one occasion, but didn't really enjoy it.

Their differences also extended to the very roots of their upbringing. Robin was the eldest of three brothers. His mum had part-time work in the local shoe factory and his father worked at the local foundry. Money, although not plentiful, had been enough for the family to secure a mortgage on a property and eventually a family car, enabling weekend visits to the coast and countryside. Robin's parents had met during one of the many local dances held in the nearby town, the same as Alice's parents. They spent many happy hours listening and dancing to the big band sound which was popular during the post war period. The music of Glen Miller enhanced the courtships of many post war couples, adding magic and hope following the trauma endured during the war years.

By contrast, Alice was raised alongside her elder brother Darren and younger sister Diane in a three-bedroom semi-detached rented house. With three young children, Alice's mum was unable to work and despite her father working seven days a week there was never enough money to save for a deposit to buy their own home. From Scottish ancestry, her father was very old fashioned in his ways. Even as the children got older, he discouraged his wife from going out to work, insisting he would provide for his family. Consequently, money was short and times were made harder when he was off work for many months following a back injury which he sustained down the coal mine. He had been a builder by trade, having worked his apprenticeship with a renowned company and earned his deed of apprenticeship on the eighth of April 1948.

However, compared to the wages from working down the coal mine with the addition of regular concessionary coal for fuel, his wage as a young experienced builder was low and not enough to support his growing family, therefore in the best interest of the family he went to work underground. When Alice was nineteen, her sister Catherine was born, much to the shock and surprise of her parents.

Her mum, despite having had three children, was not aware of the pregnancy until one month before the premature birth. Naturally, the young Catherine was adored and cherished by her parents and older siblings.

Alice always felt close to her family and despite the age gap between herself and Catherine she was always closely involved with her sister's life. When Catherine was a baby, Alice would take her to the baby clinic and regularly care for her. She was by her side on the first day at infant school and subsequently followed her sister's progress, encouraging her with her studies. Alice was so proud when she witnessed her sister receive a first class honours degree in chemistry and later a PHD.

Despite the lack of money in the family household in the early years of Alice's life, they always spent a week at the seaside every summer, enjoyed family celebrations, decent food and were well clothed, something she remembers with pride.

Alice's beloved father had died just five years previous and she still missed him so much. Many times recently she wished he was around to advise her about her current problems. At times, Alice let her mind wonder, trying to imagine what advice he would give. Maybe he could have put a male perspective on the situation, helping her to understand Robin's dilemma. Although her brother Darren had assumed the father role with his sisters since the death of their father, Alice knew he himself had problems enough and didn't want to burden him with her own worries. Robin's mum had also died in the recent past. She had died six months previous after a short illness, when his wounds were still raw from the loss of his first wife. He struggled at times to hide his grief but it was painfully obvious to see; those scars would never go away. That first cut would forever be the deepest and the death of his mum reinforced the pain.

For these reasons, Alice knew she would need to handle any future events with great sensitivity.

Now, climbing the stairs, carefully holding the hot drinks, Alice glanced to her left, where two sepia coloured photographs hung in antique silver frames. The nearer of the two showed Alice's parents on their wedding day, circa December 1948. Her mum, very slim and beautiful, of pure Anglo-Saxon ancestry, was smiling in her long gown of white Nottingham lace, her arm linked with a tall, slim, dark, curly haired young man who looked very grand indeed in his pin-striped suit. They were stood outside the village church, with its austere entrance of sculptured walls and paired gargoyles. It was the very same scene where Alice and her sister Diane had posed for their own wedding photographs years later. The whole family had been christened, married and had their funerals there and no doubt this would continue.

The far photograph was of Robin's parents, they were stood outside the local Roman Catholic church, with arms tightly linked. Robin's mum was also very slim, wearing a long white gown and carrying a huge bouquet of flowers. Beside her was a proud and happy young man.

Looking at the wedding photographs, her mind drifted back to her own wedding day, five years previous. What a wonderful day that was. Just perfect in every way. Such a happy joyful occasion when both families came together to celebrate a new beginning for Robin and Alice. A time when both Robin's parents were alive to witness their son re-marry after the loss of his beloved wife and have a chance of happiness in a new loving marriage. Sadly for Alice, her own father was not alive to walk her down the aisle and give his daughter to her new husband as he had done twenty-seven years earlier when he had proudly walked his daughter down the isle of the church he himself was married in. It was Mathew who walked his mum down the aisle to be joined in matrimony with Robin in the presence of their family and friends.

Lost in thought, Alice gently pushed open the bedroom door and placed Robin's mug of tea on his bedside table. She smiled. As usual he had rolled over to her side of the bed, cuddling the pillow where her head had previously laid. Robin once told her, it was the smell of her perfume lingering on the pillow that drew him over to her side of the king size bed. As she watched her husband peacefully sleeping, Alice grew anxious about how their lives were about to change if she remained true to herself and to the statement she had made to Robin, six months earlier on their fifth wedding anniversary. It was very rare for Alice to make such profound statements without having true commitment to her convictions and she truly hoped that Robin knew her well enough to understand and heed this.

CHAPTER TWO

The second Alice switched off the television, she knew Robin would wake up and claim he was watching the television with his eyes shut, and listening to the news. Predictably, this is exactly what happened. Without delay, Robin sat up, moving over to his side of the bed, leaving room for his wife to get back into bed with him, hoping perhaps she had changed her mind and was maybe willing to satisfy his desires. His wish to make love to his wife was short lived, as the sound of movement coming from the bedroom which backed onto theirs, signalled that Stephen, Robin's eldest son, was awake and needed the bathroom, which meant he would not be sound asleep again for some time. They both felt uncomfortable making love surrounded on all sides by Robin's grown up family. It had been like this from the moment they were married, so once again they had to take a rain check and take advantage of privacy on a future occasion. Instead, they snuggled under the duvet with their hands wrapped around the hot mugs instead of each other.

They discussed the plans for the day. Robin always helped prepare the vegetables. Today he would peel enough potatoes for ten people, just in case Mathew or Anne Marie rang to enquire if it was okay for them to join everyone for dinner. Although this rarely occurred, Alice always lived in hope. She respected their busy lives, working in the city in demanding jobs. The free time during the weekend was taken up renovating their homes, studying for further qualifications and in Anne Marie's case working in her garden, which now resembled an allotment. The garden, her pride and joy, was full of vegetables, fruit trees and blackcurrant bushes. Anne Marie was very passionate about the land and sustainability of the earth. She prided herself in being environmentally conscientious, never using insecticides or harming the wildlife. She grew fresh herbs, salads, vegetables and fruit, which being a vegetarian helped enormously with her food bills. She also wrote poetry and articles relating to her values and beliefs.

Alice always prepared a large selection of vegetables for Sunday dinner so as to suit everyone's taste. The turkey and stuffing, always popular with the family, she cooked to perfection. They never worried about dessert because Alice's mum, a super pastry cook, always came bearing a delicious home-made fruit pie, freshly prepared that morning. Not one to take advantage of other people's generosity, she never came empty handed and was extremely grateful for everything that was done to help her.

Alice enjoyed Sundays when they all sat around the big refectory table in the dining room chatting about the week's events. She loved to listen to the family banter, each of them sharing news about their respective jobs, friends and plans. However, much to her disappointment, most weeks there was some element of sibling rivalry and sullen behaviour from Robin's family. A regular bone of contention with Robin was dress code. Miraculously, just as the dinner was being served, his children would drag themselves out of bed and attempt to sit at the dining table in their pyjamas. Always this annoyed Robin, who insisted they should leave the table and return suitably dressed.

Around midday Robin drove to his old family home to collect his father. They would go to the local pub for a couple of pints of real ale before returning home for dinner. Fetching his father was a new development in the family routine. For although aged eighty-four, he was still happily driving his own car until the annual road tax and insurance was due and he announced quite out of the blue that he was hanging up his car keys for good. Both Robin and Alice were relieved to some extent as they worried that his health was beginning to limit the speed of his reactions.

Also it was less worry around constant maintenance issues. However, Robin's father found it difficult to accept that he was now dependent on his family for transport. He now relied on his sons and daughter in law to take him shopping, to their homes and any other venues necessary.

Within a month of each other, Wayne and Gary had managed to secure jobs within the same town, therefore it made sense to buy the boys a car to share for work purposes until they had saved enough to purchase one each. This proved to work well for a while, until Gary's three month trial contract was not renewed. Stephen was able to share the car at the weekends.

Fundamentally the boys were different, with personality traits that tended to clash. There had been many occasions when the volatile nature of Gary had clashed with tormenting from his brothers. The shouting and slamming of doors with days of not speaking to one another were commonplace in the household. Wayne, the younger brother by two years, was well placed in his chosen field of work as a trainee chef. He was interested in food preparation and even more interested in sampling the goods. On occasion he stood by Alice when she was preparing food, although that was the limit of his interest in the family kitchen.

Stephen, the eldest of Robin's sons, was sports mad and had studied sport science at the local college. He tended to take sides with his sister Julie and was always defending her and creating unrest between his other two brothers. Gary was an apprentice joiner, which he appeared to enjoy. These differences, along with the personality traits of other family members, created major problems, leading to family unrest and disharmony. Disagreements erupted into arguments and unrest lasting many weeks, culminating in door slamming, constant arguments and at times the use of rhetoric which would normally be X-rated.

Added to this melting pot, Mathew was totally different from Robin's boys with his serious nature and work ethos, which sometimes aggravated both Robin and his family. A lot of diplomacy was required to maintain family peace and harmony.

They both knew when they married that the path ahead would have many twists and turns.

Especially so for Alice. Her own family had been independent. Mathew had left home at nineteen to attend university, his sister Ann Marie missed him so much that six months later she joined him in his shared student accommodation and found herself a job close to the university.

Although upset at the time, Alice had grown accustomed to living alone and on her marriage to Robin this had changed dramatically as she inherited four grown up step children. From living alone and enjoying the freedom and space of her own home, she quickly had to adjust to sharing her new home with six other adults, for Mathew had planned to be living with them on a temporary basis, at least until he had saved enough money to pay off his student loan.

The most difficult relationship for Alice was with Robin's daughter Julie. At first when her father and Alice were courting she appeared happy for her father, pleased he wasn't lonely after her mum passed, enabling herself and her brothers to worry less about his wellbeing. She was only twelve years old when she lost her mum to leukaemia. This had been a traumatic, heart-wrenching experience for her at such a young tender age; an age when a young girl benefits from the education only a mum can give to a young daughter as she is approaching womanhood.

Although she was close to her aunties and her grandmothers, neither of them were able to compensate for the loss of her beloved mum. Julie had been the long awaited daughter, as a result she was a little spoiled and naturally coveted by her mum, choosing many pretty clothes and shoes, lots of treats and surprises. Unfortunately Robin was unable to continue with this, for he also had the boys' welfare to consider and, never having a sister of his own, he found himself in new territory. Alice was aware of this and although she kept her distance, she tried to fill some of the motherly gaps without appearing to be trying to replace her mum.

This was a difficult juggling act at times, for she didn't wish to offend anyone or upset her own children. It was like treading on eggshells at times, which became very exhausting.

Following the death of his wife, Robin needed to return to work. The company he worked for had been very accommodating and understanding, allowing him much needed extended sick leave.

With the help of his parents, family life continued. His mum helped with the washing and household chores. His dad collected the children and drove them to school. When Robin worked late, his parents prepared the evening meal and stayed with the children until Robin arrived home from work. Later, when Robin met Alice, she would spend the weekend at the house helping out with the household duties and cooking Sunday lunch for everyone. She realised that if she wanted to spend time with Robin then this was the only solution. She recognised how Robin needed to be there for his family but at the same time understood his desire to be with her. How difficult it must have been for him and how emotionally painful at times.

Having lost their mum, the children were naturally treated with great kindness and affection to the point of pampering at times. Unfortunately, they were not encouraged to help with the household tasks or to keep their own rooms clean and tidy. In addition, granddad was at their beck and call. He drove them everywhere at their request, even very short distances for which he was expected to drive from the opposite side of town where he lived and transport them a very short distance into town, rather than to go by the local bus, which meant getting out of bed ten minutes earlier.

Alice stood by and observed this with a heavy heart.

When they all began living together in the new family home, this lack of early encouragement created an uncomfortable situation for Alice. As Julie got older she became increasingly stubborn about helping around the home or keeping her own room clean and tidy. The boys also did very little to help. Mathew, true to his word, had only lived with the family for thirteen months, having saved a small deposit for a new build. This kind of attitude was unfamiliar to Alice. She had always prided herself on keeping a clean well organised home: clean, crisp white bed linen and towels, food served at appropriate times, sat at a table not straight from a plate balanced on a lap while watching the television. Her own children Mathew and Anne Marie had both been encouraged to keep their own bedrooms clean and tidy and to help around the home with simple chores. When Alice worked late, her daughter prepared a meal for mum, both Mathew and Anne Marie made sure the bins were empty and the sink clean for when their mum came home. As such it became very annoying for Alice to arrive home when Robin was working late every other week and find his family laying on the sofas while in the kitchen the sink was full of greasy pots and pans, the waste bin overflowing onto the floor and a laundry room with piles of dirty clothes including stained underwear on the floor, waiting for Alice, the laundry fairy, to wash. For some strange reason, they waited for one another to bring a week's worth of washing from their rooms so it could be dumped in a pile on the floor.

The dirty underwear of Julie's, thrown on the floor in full view of everyone, embarrassed Alice who gently tried to dissuade this type of behaviour, but her advice fell on deaf ears.

The problem for Alice was rooted in the fact that when she married, their father she vowed to herself that she would be careful not to try and replace their mum, therefore allowing Robin to take full responsibility with herself taking a back seat. She knew it would be difficult to share Robin, after all he had been all theirs for their entire life and there would be some degree of resentment. She had anticipated a certain lack of co-operation to a point, but not to the extent of getting out of control… Alice was ruminating on these issues when she heard the sound of the kitchen door click open and in walked her mum with a cheery smile on her lovely face. She was carefully carrying a big oval dish full of apple crumble. It must have still been warm and fresh from the oven for it was cushioned in a thick and pretty tea towel. The aroma from the cooked apples filled the air with a warm comforting smell, reminding Alice of her childhood sat around the big kitchen table with her brother and sister eagerly awaiting dessert.

"How are things?" her mum enquired. "Is anyone up yet?" She knew how the situation was with respect to the frustration her daughter was feeling and how it was gradually wearing her down and affecting her health and happiness. Her mum observed that, as usual, Alice was at the kitchen sink with her apron on, trying to be the perfect wife and step mother, hoping to please everyone else with no thought for her own happiness.

Recently her brother Darren had expressed his concerns for his sister and spoke to his mum of how he felt Alice was doing too much, working all week and dancing around Robin and his family on her days off, instead of enjoying her own quality time pursuing activities she herself enjoyed. There had been a time when he himself was going through a difficult time and Alice was there for him. Occasionally, she would accompany him on a long walk around the local woods, a place where he felt a free spirit once more, a place of calm and tranquillity, enabling him to clear his head of his own worries. Alice was always there to listen to his problems as she had with her younger sister Dianne. They shared an appreciation of the outdoors, wildlife and the clear fresh air. Darren had a special interest in birds and Alice, always a good listener, gave him the opportunity to talk about his passion for ornithology.

Alice had opened her home up to her sister, Dianne, when her own marriage was in difficulty.

Her sister eventually moved in with her. She had taken her under her wing and eventually introduced her to Paul, who later became her second husband. Yes, Alice had helped her sister in a number of ways. On her own recommendation and by pulling a few strings in the right places, Alice managed to get her sister a job at the hospital as a health care assistant despite not having any previous experience. Dianne remained there to this day, enjoying her work at the hospital.

Darren held his sister in high esteem with great admiration and respect as he did for all of his sisters. Being the only boy in the family, he assumed the responsibility of their father when he died and Darren had every intention of keeping more than a close eye on all of his sisters. Alice was his priority at the moment.

Alice's mum was also not happy with the way Robin's family were taking advantage. Her daughter had been insistent that when she married Robin, it would be a true partnership in every possible way, which included a joint bank account, investing everything they earned from the day of their marriage and both having free access to use the money appropriately. Being sensitive to Robin's earned income before their marriage, Alice suggested that Robin always keep this separate out of respect to his first wife, therefore any previous investments they had made together were his alone. After all she had also worked and contributed to their joint income and subsequent savings.

Alice however, only received half of the combined savings and half value of the home, with fifty percent belonging to her first husband. Despite this, she had been very careful with her money and was never concerned about finances. The team ethos Alice had with Robin concerned her mum. She knew her daughter earned a good wage and she also knew that despite Robin's children working, they did not contribute at all towards their keep, neither did they buy the occasional bottle of wine or beer; they systematically took everything for granted. She considered that they were living in the equivalent of a five-star hotel, with a chauffeur driven car thrown in. To Alice's mum this was unheard of. Her own children started paying towards their keep from the moment they drew their first wage packet until the day they left home. She remembered Alice proudly handing over to her parents her first wage packet at the age of fifteen. Not old enough to start her nurse training, but with a keen interest in medicine, she had secured a job at the local chemist shop, helping with dispensing and stock control. How she had enjoyed that job, despite the low wage.

That first week and for many weeks after, her wages, were three pounds, eight shillings and eleven pence weekly. Alice was allowed to keep the eight shillings and eleven pence, giving three pounds towards the household costs. Having been raised in the kind of environment that fostered respect and good family values, her mum could not understand how Alice had allowed this to go on for so long. Her own grandchildren Mathew and Anne Marie were both working in two jobs to make ends meet and pay their mortgage. Indeed, there was a time when her granddaughter worked full time Monday to Friday, worked the weekend in a hotel as a waitress and still managed two evening shifts a week at the Post Office sorting department. Alice's own children went without holidays and had very few luxuries in life and yet their mum was helping to provide free gratis for Robin's children. Despite this, she knew it would only be a matter of time before her daughter would undoubtedly try and instigate some major changes. Any decisions Alice made, her family would be with her one hundred percent. A very close knit family, together they supported one another with steely determination and true grit.

Alice's mum opened a kitchen drawer and took out an apron. She smiled. On a visit to London one weekend during her post-divorce period, Alice had visited Harrods department store and chosen a gift for each member of the family. Her gift to her mum had been the apron with Harrods embellished on the pocket. She put the apron on in readiness to help Alice with the final preparation of the meal.

As the aroma from the cooked turkey drifted up to the next floor, there was a vague sound of movement, evidence that Robin's family were finally getting out of their beds. It was nearly half past two. A few minutes later as promised, Robin and his father came home from his lunch time visit to the local pub. Within minutes, knowing the meal was about to be served, down the stairs trooped all of them, wearing pyjamas and obviously unwashed. Immediately, Robin told his children not to come to the table until they were properly dressed. Wayne promptly made his way upstairs to do as his father had bid him. Gary, however, began a verbal assault, insisting he was properly dressed and not wearing pyjamas, but lounge bottoms and a tee shirt. A battle ensued. Alice took a deep breath and waited patiently to see what the outcome would be this lunchtime, because sure enough the battle would continue into a full scale war. Julie and Stephen joined in with their brother in the protest, then slowly and deliberately stomped up the stairs and emerged a minute later wearing yesterday's crumpled dirty jeans over the top of their pyjamas and equally dirty crumpled tee shirts. No one was going to get the better of them.

Robin's father, embarrassed by yet another ridiculous show from his grandchildren who were old enough to know better, disappeared outside to have a cigarette. He stood, sheltered just outside the door, lighting his cigarette and contemplating the situation. His own sons had more respect, they would never behave in such a disgraceful manner. He looked around at the surrounding scene. The tubs and urns were showing evidence of the approaching spring. The bulbs were pushing their way towards the light. Little piles of dry old leaves were being blown around in circles around his feet. The dustbin looked to be full, which was hardly surprising with the amount of food the family got through in a week. At the side of the house wall he noticed a row of stub marks burnt into the brickwork were Julie deliberately stubbed out her cigarettes despite being asked not to do so on a number of occasions. He carefully put his cigarette into the bin just as Robin called him in for dinner.

Robin assisted Alice and her mum in transferring the food from the kitchen to the dining table. All of the food was served in big tureens to allow for personal choice and quantity. No sooner had they started to help themselves to dinner, when Gary marched into the dining room having changed into jeans and a tee shirt. Within two minutes a further debate began, developing into a full scale argument until everyone had their say. Alice had worked hard to provide a nice meal for everyone. Her mum also had put in a lot of effort with the dessert. Is it worth the effort? thought Alice as she listened to the constant bickering which was reaching fever pitch with voices being raised to a deafening pitch. It was akin to being in a primary school playground.

"Put your dummies away!" shouted Alice above the racket. "I've heard quite enough for one day."

Surprisingly, this did the trick and they settled down to eat their meal in a more civilized manner.

This is ridiculous, thought Alice. This was her home as well as Robin's and yet his family had completely taken over, causing mayhem and chaos on a daily basis. She didn't really want this at her age and neither should Robin be tolerating it.

Julie was the first to finish her meal, which was probably strategic, for she promptly flopped lazily onto the sofa, laid fully stretched across the entire length and grabbed the remote control with a view to taking over the television for the rest of the day. Anyone who dared to complain would receive a constant battering of rhetoric reminiscent of a Gatling gun in full battle. When everyone else had finished eating, Robin's father very cautiously asked Julie to help with the clearing away and to help wash the dishes. Alice and her mum waited for the reply, knowing full well what the answer would be, for neither of them had ever seen her lift a finger to help Alice.

Indeed, she had never even offered to help in any way, perhaps by making a hot drink for Alice when she came in from work or even when Alice had been ill consequently, as usual, Robin overcompensated and said he would clear away the dishes while Alice prepared the custard to accompany the apple crumble. Meanwhile, the boys also made themselves comfortable around the television, none of them offering to help. All of them with full bellies, having just risen from their mattresses, had no intention of any kind of physical activity, especially anything which involved effort. Peace did not reign for long. Very soon they began to argue about which television program to watch. Julie wanted to view the Walt Disney Channel to watch cartoons. This was a trait that Alice had been concerned about for some time; she was worried that Julie was hanging on to her childhood and did not want to grow up.

Alice wondered about the deep rooted reasons for this and was concerned that she was understandably hanging on to her past, when her mum was alive and she was her adored little girl. Gary wanted to watch *Top Gear* a program about cars while Stephen and Wayne were showing off because they wanted to watch football. Alice knew that Robin probably would prefer to watch football himself but wouldn't say as much. The arguing went on for some time with each one calling the others selfish among other expletives until Robin finally took the remote control from his daughter's hand, put it in his own pocket and informed them that he would decide for the majority. This did not go down well, each of them shouting at Robin and in amazingly close ranks; for the first time that morning they were agreeing with one another. Alice's mum and Robin's father who were of the old school, possessing sound values and beliefs could not understand why Robin had allowed his children to be so disrespectful.

Meanwhile, in the kitchen Alice was beginning to feel stressed. Her heart was beating fast and hard in her chest, her mouth was dry and she felt unwell.

Her head was in turmoil. She could see no end to this, no light at the end of the tunnel, and this would go on and on forever until her relationship with Robin was ruined just like the fallen autumn fruit laying on the ground to spoil.

Alice mulled over the conversations she had shared with Robin about their own family lives and how he and his brothers had lived at home with their parents supporting them. It had been marriage that had instigated their move from the nest, but they had all been in a good financial position, enabling the purchase of a home of their own.

Alice rested her weary head against her hands, supporting her tense aching neck. How could she cope for another five years or more? It could be even longer, thought Alice. After all, why would they want to move out? They had no responsibilities, made no financial contribution and everything was done for them without lifting a finger. They came and went as they pleased, invited friends to stay over in their bedrooms whenever they wanted. Every penny they earned was spent on pleasure, going to night clubs, smoking, drinking and buying the latest CDs and fashionable clothes. Yes, they had a good life, why change things? Some mornings when Alice woke up and went into the kitchen to make herself a drink, she would find a stranger or two asleep on the floor in a sleeping bag. Sometimes Julie had two or three girls sleeping in bed with her top to toe. The boys also invited friends to stay over in their rooms or they slept on the sofa in the lounge and conservatory, much to the annoyance of Alice, especially when the rooms smelled of sweaty clothes and cheesy trainers. Alice did not approve of this behaviour and felt that Robin and she were being disrespected. The root of the problem lay at the very beginning of their marriage. Alice, sensitive to the loss of their mum, did not want to come across as taking over her role, so she had encouraged Robin to take full responsibility for his family in as much as the discipline and encouraging good behaviour and values.

But this was not working. In retrospect, she wondered if this had been a sensible idea, perhaps if she had involved herself more, even at the risk of being labelled a wicked step mother, things may have been a little different now. Was it too late to take shared control of the reins, even more worryingly, would Robin allow it?

Robin came into the kitchen and he gently wrapped his strong warm arms around her tiny waist, cuddling her tenderly. Her heart began to melt, she loved Robin so much, but was that enough to sustain her through the next few years? Would her love for him support her through every crisis? Time would tell.

"It won't be long now," he gently said. "We will soon be relaxing in Portugal, you'll see, we will have a great time with Kay and Gavin. You can relax and read to your heart's content, we will have such a good time." The pleading and desperation in his voice created a lump in her throat and she felt tears well up in her eyes. A knot of tissue tightened up in her gut, squeezing tighter and tighter making her gasp. "Are you alright?" said Robin. Trying to keep her voice calm, Alice replied that she was and promptly went outside to shake the table cloth. As she did so she glanced at the cigarette stub marks on the wall. Alice knew full well that when they returned from Portugal, the number of stub marks would have trebled, the kitchen sink would be greasy and dirty and full of pots. The work surfaces would be surrounded in crumbs and burn marks and the waste bin overflowing. Alice took in a deep breath of fresh air, hoping to alleviate the overwhelming feeling of nausea that overcame her. She always worried about her precious home while away. Frequently the doors had been left unlocked all day and night, putting their home at risk from opportunistic burglary. For this reason, she had a lock put on their bedroom door and the downstairs bedroom where she stored her jewellery and important documents.

Around four thirty, Alice gently called her mum who was sat comfortably on the sofa with Robin's dad, reminiscing about their past memories, enjoying spending time with a companion who understood the old ways. Although worlds apart in as much as their childhoods and experiences in life, they found a common ground to share memories. Memories of the special times they shared with their spouses and the pain they experienced of their loss. It was good for both Alice and Robin to observe their parents enjoying the hospitality and company of their home. Both of them felt great respect and love for their parents and shared a great sadness that they had both lost their soul mates.

Alice's mum said she was ready to go home and enquired if Alice would call in and have a coffee with her before she left. Alice knew this was because her mum hated going into the quiet house having been surrounded by company all afternoon. She called to Robin explaining she may be a little while. Her mum thanked Robin for his hospitality and kindness and wished good health to his father. She called upstairs to Robin's family, but they didn't hear her call, for their music was loud and drowned out her farewell. They were oblivious to the hard work and effort their dad and Alice had spent in time and energy to provide a family meal which they hoped everyone would enjoy. On the drive back to her mum's, they spoke of the afternoon events. Her mum suggested that perhaps Alice and Robin should take some Sundays off and pursue an activity they both enjoy. Maybe a walk along a canal which they both liked or maybe a day in the countryside or at the coast, followed by a meal instead of Alice spending her day off at the kitchen sink. Alice smiled. In her heart she knew that it would be a rare Sunday that she would let her mum and father in law eat alone in their respective homes, as it was doubtful that any of their other siblings would rush to invite their parent for Sunday lunch.

They arrived at her mum's and after assisting her out of the car, Alice walked with her mum down the sloping path which lead to the front door. This was the home were Alice was born and raised. This would be the place her mum would live out the rest of her life.

She felt a lump in her throat, a deep sadness overwhelmed her and Alice knew she would not let her mum down. For as long as she lived Alice would be there for her mum. Before entering the house, Alice checked around the back to make sure the house was secure. This had become a ritual since the house had been broken in to and her mum's jewellery and other personal possessions had been stolen two years previous while she was at Darren's house for Mother's Day.

Fortunately, Darren was with his mum at the moment of realisation of the burglary and it appeared the culprits had left only seconds earlier as the security lights were still on. They had broken in through the back window leaving a trail of destruction behind them. At the time and for many months following the event, her mum was very upset and shaken. The loss of confidence in the security and safety of her own home became a real issue for her mum. For the first time since the loss of her husband, she felt old and vulnerable. However, the police had been very supportive and the insurance company fulfilled all of the promises made in their policy. Gradually, with the support of her family and friends, Alice's mum gained the confidence to leave her home, knowing that the house was now alarmed, owing to a local initiative which provided house alarms for the local elderly residents.

Alice followed her mum into the familiar kitchen…Memories of childhood flashed through her mind. The familiar kitchen table which Alice dreaded sitting around at meal times with the family. She remembered how her lack of appetite and subsequent picking at her food created much anguish for her parents. Alice would chew and chew her food until she was able to swallow a morsel. At times Alice would store food in her mouth then excuse herself to the toilet to spit out the whole mouthful. These days this was not such a problem. By the time Alice had reached adolescence, her appetite was as good as anyone else's.

While her mum took off her coat, Alice filled the kettle and collected the coffee mugs. Very soon the coffee was ready and with their hands enveloped around the warm mugs they sat contently at the kitchen table. Her mum, with a deep sigh, told Alice that she was very concerned about her, for she looked so very tired and drained. She went on to explain her worry about Alice's health and enquired if she had considered her long term happiness and health. Alice tried to reassure her mum, informing her that very soon she would instigate some changes at great emotional and financial expense to herself and Robin which she now felt was her only option. Alice felt she was trapped in a corner awaiting the first available escape route which opened. This she did not tell her mum for fear of further worry.

They chatted comfortably together for some time, putting the world to rights and discussing family matters. Soon it was time for Alice to leave. She hugged her mum and reminded her to lock up securely. Alice hated leaving her mum alone. This was the worst part of the day for her.

Seeing her mum alone at the door left her feeling so very sad, a sadness which would have been so much worse if it wasn't for the knowledge that her brother and two sisters would call to see her mum in the week and she herself would visit her on Wednesday and take her shopping followed by a visit to the cemetery to pay respect to her father. Every Wednesday except for when Alice was away on holiday, she took her mum to the grave of her father. Alice got no comfort from this but her mum drew much comfort and a feeling of calm and peace following the visit. Her mum sometimes pointed to the space on the gravestone which was the area deliberately left for her own epitaph to be written. This always upset Alice who couldn't bear to think about the loss of her mum. Alice often thought of her own mortality and if not careful she could get quite depressed with such thoughts. Her main worry was her children and how they would have to wait for their rightful inheritance as the majority of her money was tied up in the property which Robin and his family would need to live in. Although she planned to write a will leaving all of her personal money and possessions to her children, her share of the house value was a reflection of her life's work and although Robin could sell up and buy a smaller property therefore releasing their share, somehow Alice could not see this happening. In addition to her brother and sisters visiting her mum, Robin also called in for a chat and a cup of tea when he was on a late afternoon shift. Sometimes her mum's two brothers also called in and her sister if she was in the area. Alice knew her mum was well thought of as she made all of her visitors feel so welcome.

But no one was there in the morning when she awoke. No one to wish good morning to or good night before she climbed into her empty bed. For this reason, Robin had tried to persuade her mum to have a dog for companionship and security, but she was too house proud to consider this and after a while Robin gave up trying to persuade her.

Driving home, Alice once again thought of the forth coming holiday that she and Robin so desperately needed. Instead of feeling excited at the anticipation of the holiday, she felt troubled, a feeling she had discussed with Robin just a few days earlier when she had asked Robin to speak to his family and give them a gentle reminder of the house ground rules of no parties while they were away and to remember to keep the house clean and safe. Alice began to fret, for she knew it made no difference for whatever their father said to his family, it would fall on deaf ears. In the past they had passed off a party as just having a gathering of friends around for a few drinks, a game of poker and to listen to music. Alice did not mind a few friends around, after all she remembered what it was like to be young and did not deny them the joy of friendship, providing it was a couple of friends and not a houseful of rowdy teenagers.

The days prior to the holiday she busied herself preparing for the holiday and making arrangements with her friends. She washed and ironed the holiday clothes and packed them neatly into the suitcase. It will be nice to be wearing light and pretty summer clothes again, thought Alice, instead of the heavy winter clothes. A smile reached her lips as she thought of the warm sunshine on her face after what had been a long and miserable winter. Alice tried to feel light hearted and excited as she packed the sun cream and Robin's panama hat, but she couldn't lift her mood, it was stuck in a groove of worry and dread. As usual Robin was more concerned with filling the freezer and fridge full of ready prepared food for his family, who would each cook their own food without consideration to the others in fear they might have to do a little more of the work. Occasionally when it suited him, Stephen would cook a spaghetti Bolognese, leaving some for his brothers and sister to share, but then they argued about who would clear away the dishes. Consequently, once the dishwasher was full of dirty pots with remnants of dried food attached, the remainder of the dirty dishes were left in the sink as they could not agree who the dirty pots belonged to. Robin also made sure there were plenty of toilet rolls in stock, which when empty they would drop the cardboard rolls on the floor later claiming "it wasn't me." Flushing the toilet also seemed to be a task too much, resulting in toilet bowls only seen in public convenience spots.

CHAPTER THREE

On the morning of their departure, Alice was suddenly overcome with a sense of fear and worry.

It was almost a gut feeling of something dreadful happening. She had often spoken to Robin about their responsibility to the family in the event of their death and the need to make the situation a little easier by leaving a will so that their estate would not be dragged through the long laborious process of probate. Robin had always dismissed the idea for reasons Alice could not begin to understand she herself preferred to be organised, especially in matters as important as the children's welfare.

She could not begin to imagine the utter chaos for the children of arranging funerals and financial settlements, certainly arguments would ensue because without a will from either parent, Mathew being the eldest would try to take on the role and responsibility and may even inherit the estate which would naturally result in Robin's family feeling resentful and bitter.

Alice had made enquiries about making a will and was surprised to learn that in the absence of a will, if both parties died in an accident at the same time, it would be deemed as Alice dying second because she was the younger of the two, therefore leaving Mathew the eldest as the sole beneficiary. Robin always refused to even consider writing a will and although she reminded him many times, he buried his head in the sand, refusing and saying it was not necessary, Alice found this all very frustrating and decided that if Robin did not write one soon then she would have no alternative other than to go to a solicitor alone. With this in mind, she quickly wrote a letter detailing her own last wishes and addressed this to Mathew. Alice left this on the bedside table in Mathew's old room on the ground level of the house.

This was the room where she stored her jewellery and important documents. A room which was kept locked and secure at all times, unless in use for a guest.

Later on during the journey to the airport, Alice texted Mathew to inform him of the letter. He occasionally stayed over in his old room when he had an evening meeting in the area and for this reason she had given him a key in case he needed to stay over while they were away on holiday.

Having done this, she felt satisfied that everything was complete and all else was out of her control. She made a mental promise to herself that at no time during the holiday would she worry Robin or spoil the ambience by discussing the problems at home. Robin deserved a break as much as she and nothing was going to spoil it.

They flew to Faro Airport in Portugal and spent an idyllic week in fabulous surroundings. The apartment which their friends had purchased three years earlier was exactly as Kay had described. It was surrounded by lush vegetation and exotic plants. The swimming pool was well equipped with pool furniture, a poolside bar and shady areas ideal for relaxing and reading the many novels which herself and Kay planned to read. Their husbands were happy to admire the passing attractions with regular visits to the poolside bar. Very soon they were relaxed and enjoying each other's company. In the evenings they strolled into the town to choose a place to eat and share a bottle of wine. There were plenty of interesting restaurants, but their favourites were the seafood restaurants serving fish produce, grilled on huge charcoal barbecues and served with home-made crusty bread and side salad.

Despite Alice's best intentions not to worry about back home, Kay brought up the subject one afternoon while the men were having a game of golf. She told Alice how concerned she was for her friend and how she had always thought that Alice may have taken too much on with Robin and his children and how lucky he was to have Alice as his wife as not many women whose own children were independent would have taken on such a mammoth task. Alice knew this of course and despite Robin's claim that his love for her was equal with his children, she had made a pledge to herself that she would never drive a wedge between Robin and his family. Not because she was afraid of the answer, more because it would be unfair on Robin. After all, she had made her wedding vows and would honour the promises made. She knew only too well the feeling of betrayal as she had experienced this in her first marriage and remembered the pain of it. She loved Robin and knew he loved her, but his children were of his own flesh as Anne Marie and Mathew were hers and she would never wish to cause ill feeling which could not be repaired.

Kay was a good friend, they had been through so much together, helping to heal the wounds of their broken marriages, fetching each other's children from school, getting each other's washing in on rainy days and putting it through the tumble dryer, helping with birthday parties and barbecues and supporting each other constantly.

Alice told Kay she had always been prepared for the difficulties ahead but wasn't expecting such a long haul and now she could see no light at the end of the tunnel, not even a glimmer of hope on the horizon. The boys were well old enough to leave home even if it meant sharing a rented flat. They needed to learn to live independently. Alice had left home and married at twenty-one and her sister had been nineteen, both of them with a spirit of independence and not wishing to be dependent on their parents. The boys were already in their mid-twenties and had no interest in leaving home. But why would they want to leave? Robin allowed them to come and go as they pleased, they enjoyed free board and lodgings and no responsibilities. Alice turned uncomfortably on the sun lounger, she was feeling the tension rise up her back and into her shoulders and neck. She decided to approach the subject with Robin on helping the boys to move out. She would bring up the subject when she felt the time was right as she had learned a long time ago that the timing was paramount to a successful outcome and with Robin and this was no exception. She had to choose the right moment when he may be receptive, otherwise he would once again bury his head in the sand, stop listening hoping the problem would disappear.

The afternoon sun began to help Alice relax. She savoured the warmth and allowed herself to drift off to sleep for a short while, blocking out all thoughts of step children and relationships. A moment's respite for her troubled mind. She awoke to find Robin resting on the sunbed beside her. He looked happy and content, having enjoyed his game of golf.

The week flew by too quickly and soon they were waving each other goodbye with the men grumbling to each other about starting work on Monday and the women complaining about the amount of washing and ironing facing them over the coming days. But Alice concealed a further nagging worry. What would her beautiful home look like? Would there be a pile of dirty dishes in the sink? Overflowing bins and the house smelling of stale tobacco and sweaty trainers? Would there be smelly sleeping bags in the conservatory? Chances were, all of those nagging worries would probably turn into reality.

Back to reality, thought Alice as she and Robin entered the back door of their home. The moment she crossed the threshold, Alice knew all was not well. The familiar tension began to creep through her body, tightening every sinew in her recently refreshed body, like vines creeping up a tree she felt the squeezing and pressure as her neck and shoulders became tense and her head began to ache. Robin put down the suitcases and with his coat still on, began clearing away the greasy dishes from the sink, followed by a wipe down of the filthy sticky work surfaces which Alice had left sparkling clean. He checked inside the dishwasher which was crammed full of dirty pots, Robin put in a wash tablet and set to heavy duty wash.

Meanwhile, Alice emptied the overflowing kitchen bin in which the contents had been pushed and pressed down so much in order to cram more in to avoid emptying, resulting in Alice having an almighty struggle to release the liner from the bin. Fortunately, the contents didn't fall through due to the durability of the liner. She collected the empty toilet rolls from the downstairs bathroom and proceeded to the upstairs bathroom to repeat the task. The toilet upstairs had not been flushed, revealing the ablutions of Mr. or Mrs. nobody. Alice proceeded to get out the bleach and give the toilet a good scrub, and she still hadn't taken off her coat. She returned downstairs to the cloak room to hang up her coat, feeling ready to cry at any moment, but Alice did not, and very rarely cried; no she kept a stiff upper lip while all of the time anger was rising up inside her like a volcano about to erupt. She would not allow a tsunami of tears to flow down her cheeks, she would not break down. In the conservatory were two empty sleeping bags and an old sweat stained pillow.

Despite the cool air she opened the windows to blow away the smell of stale tobacco, the faint whiff of cannabis or skunk and the smell of sweaty feet. Evidence of visitors staying over. Alice may as well have spoken to the wall for all of the good it had done when she specifically requested that no visitors were to stay and no parties were to take place. No respect, thought Alice. Robin offered to put the kettle on to make them a drink but he discovered there was not a drop of milk in the fridge, in fact there was no bread either and from the look of the cupboards, the whole street had been fed.

Robin was also dismayed and offered to go shopping and fetch a few supplies. When Robin left, Alice sat down at the kitchen table. Looking around her lovely kitchen, she leaned forward and rested her head in her hands. Alice felt weary and very sad. Her heart was heavy and beating so fast she could feel the pounding in her neck, causing her face to burn hot. The rising anxiety gave rise to beads of sweat forming on her forehead and her hands turning cold and clammy.

ENOUGH! She said to herself. Enough is enough.

Later that evening when they settled down together on the sofa watching the television, Alice spoke to Robin about how unhappy she felt that they were being disrespected and taken advantage of. She expressed her fears that the boys would never leave home until something changed which would encourage them to move of their own free will.

"Please speak to them," implored Alice. "Please help and encourage them to understand that life is not a free ride and that being an adult involves taking responsibility and leaving the nest. How can I respect your family when they behave in this way?" pleaded Alice.

Robin held his head forward and rubbed his tired, strained eyes. He pushed his hair from his forehead and Alice's heart ached for him. The expression on her husband's face was of anxiety and pain, a man torn, thought Alice. "I agree things need to change and paying towards their keep would be a start, but I cannot ask them for board," pleaded Robin. "I just can't do it. Will you do it for me, please?" Alice was astounded. This was not the response she had hoped for.

Even worse, was her disappointment in Robin.

For the first time since meeting her husband, Alice thought of him as a weak man and for this she was ashamed to be thinking such a thing of the man she loved. Realisation dawned on her. She knew that any changes within the family would have to be instigated by herself and by default, she would be the villain. The reality of the situation resulted in a deep ache within her heart.

Alice felt nausea rising up into her throat. Not wishing to let Robin be aware of how his statement had affected her, she gently and quietly left the room, without responding to Robin's defeatist attitude. Alice needed a familiar voice. A loving and understanding conversation. Both Mathew and Anne Marie managed to lift her spirits on previous occasions.

The sound of their voices always had a calming effect and now there was no better time than to ring one of them for a chat. Needing to be alone, she went upstairs to her bedroom, closed the door and rang Mathew on his mobile phone. Thankfully he answered. Alice told him of the lovely time they had and how relaxing the holiday had been for both of them. She told him of her unhappiness at the state of the house on their return and how the whole situation was getting her down. Mathew informed his mum that he had called round one evening during the week, finding half a dozen men sat around the dining room table playing poker, drinking, smoking and playing loud music.

Julie had friends in her bedroom drinking and smoking and getting their make up on for a night on the town. When Alice enquired if Mathew had found the letter she had left him in his old room downstairs he sounded surprised. Mathew said he had followed his mum's instructions with respect to coming to the house to collect the letter, in fact it had been the sole purpose of his visit, but the letter was nowhere to be found and in his wisdom had not discussed this with anyone, to avoid confrontation and in case his mum had been mistaken with her instructions.

Her heart began to thump once again and she felt a tightness in her chest. This could only mean more trouble. This time they had gone too far. "What are you going to do about this?" enquired Mathew. "Do you want me to deal with it? After all, the letter was sealed and addressed to me, in a locked room which theoretically doesn't have access." Alice knew that her son was angry and also he had a great feeling of responsibility towards his mum, but she didn't want him involved, it would do no good except cause ill feeling and as usual the ranks would be closed against Mathew just like in the past. She knew he would retaliate with a great passion for which she was proud of him, but on this occasion she reassured her son she would deal with it and to please trust her with this. The conversation finished, she quietly replaced the receiver and decided the best thing for her health and wellbeing at present was to soak away her tensions in a hot bath.

The smell of the lavender bath oil and the fragrance from the candle diffused through the air creating a heady humidity which quite overwhelmed her and Alice began to feel nauseous. She opened the bathroom window and breathed deeply, taking in the sharp cool air, filling her lungs and clearing her head. Feeling better, she carefully climbed into the bath and, resting her head against the warm ceramic bath, Alice allowed the warm fragrant water to bathe and sooth her tense body. The bathing complete and with a thick white bath sheet around her, Alice stood on the landing and called down to Robin that she was going to bed for an early night. She tied to read for a while but found it difficult to concentrate and kept reading the same lines over and over. Eventually she gave up. At some point, against all odds, Alice must have drifted off to sleep, for she was disturbed by a noise from downstairs. Gary, Stephen, Wayne and Julie had arrived home, they had all been out on the town together. She glanced at the clock, it was three am.

Robin slept soundly beside her, undisturbed. But Alice could not sleep. She knew they were all drunk. They were talking and laughing loudly. She heard a mobile phone ring, followed by an argumentative rhetoric peppered with expletives. The oven door creaked and the sound of oven trays clattered. A tray fell onto the floor making a loud crash and still Robin continued to sleep. The sound of the fridge and freezer doors opening and closing wound her up, knowing they were helping themselves to the contents, possibly even something she had planned to use for a meal in the week.

The arguing continued and gradually became louder. The arguing transferred from the caller to include all four of them. Alice tossed and turned until she couldn't take any more. Throwing off the bed covers she jumped out of bed, stood at the top of the stairs then, quite unlike Alice, bellowed downstairs, "Shut the fuck up, your dad and I have to be up early for work in the morning, unlike some people!" At this point, Robin finally woke up, jumped out of bed wearing just his boxer shorts, ran down the stairs and finally got involved. A major argument ensued. Each of them blaming the other, until Robin came back to bed and very quickly fell asleep having told his wife he had dealt with it. However, Alice was not so fortunate. She tossed and turned until five o'clock in the morning when she thought she could smell something burning. The smoke alarms hadn't been triggered but she had a gut feeling something was wrong. Alice quickly ran down the stairs, both the lounge and kitchen lights were on and the smell of burning drifted from the kitchen.

Horrified, she entered the kitchen to be greeted by a haze of blue smoke which originated from the oven. She opened the oven door releasing a large cloud of smoke, which drifted up the stairs and finally set off the smoke alarm waking the rest of the household except Julie who was still fast asleep in a drunken stupor on the lounge sofa. Inside the oven were four beef burgers burnt to cinders which she had decided to cook before collapsing on the sofa. Alice was furious. She turned the oven off and opened all of the windows to let in some fresh air. The boys called downstairs to enquire what was happening and Robin eventually came downstairs and, finding his daughter in a stupor on the sofa snoring and dribbling saliva from her mouth onto the cushions, he woke her up and packed her off to her own bed. Alice had no strength left to argue and felt so weary and deflated that she dismissed Robin's affectionate hug, leaving him to close the windows and clear away his daughter's mess.

Looking tired and strained when she arrived at work the next day, Alice informed her colleagues of her difficulties back home. Robin would consider this as disloyal but Alice's own philosophy was that sharing her trouble would help her colleagues understand if she was not her usual cheery self and she knew they would rally around and support her, which is exactly what happened. She was provided with regular coffee and advice throughout the day which she greatly appreciated. The sleepless night was muddling her brain as she constantly mulled over the episode of Mathew's missing letter. How had someone entered the locked room? The only rational conclusion was that someone had made a duplicate key for whatever reason, perhaps to provide a room so their friends could stay over.

There were two divan beds in the room which Alice had insisted on in case both of her children needed to stay over at the same time. This suggestion hadn't been well accepted at the time with Robin and his family, who wanted to use this room as a computer/play room. However, Alice had put her foot down on this occasion. She had sold her family home and owned half the home she shared with Robin. The majority of the furniture and furnishings belonged to Alice and yet Robin's family had the use of four bedrooms and yet still wanted a further room. Alice made it clear, the home was for her family also and a room should be set aside for them, even though it was one between them.

So, whoever entered the room had taken the letter addressed to Mathew and most probably read the contents, which no doubt would infuriate the reader, for Alice had left strict instructions on how her portion of the property and estate was to be shared between her children.

As it turned out, Alice did not have to bring up the uncomfortable subject because Julie did it for her. Later that day when she arrived home, her facial expression was of anger and indignation, which Alice found surprising as she did not appear at all remorseful of the event the previous night. Her tone of voice was arrogant as she insisted to speak with her father alone and in private.

Alice was alerted, for this signalled trouble to be sure. This wasn't the first time this had happened. The four of them often excluded Alice, keeping her out of the loop. Robin reinforced the situation by not sharing information with her. On one occasion when Alice had enquired about Gary and Julie going away for the weekend to a concert, Julie had snapped back at her saying it was none of her business what they were doing over the weekend. In fact, Alice only wanted to know if they would be home for Sunday dinner so she knew what size joint to buy.

Robin jumped to attention at the demand in his daughter's voice as he recognised she was in no mood to be kept waiting otherwise he would get the backlash of her temper later.

Alice went into the kitchen, giving them both space and privacy. She heard no raised voices, so assumed that Robin had somehow placated his daughter... Julie seemed satisfied with the outcome, for she had a smug expression on her face for the entire evening. Alice did not bother to enquire from Robin what the conversation had been about. After all, if he wanted his wife to know, he would tell her. Otherwise, let sleeping dogs lie.

But, sleeping dogs were not left to lie, the jealous cats had risen. Apparently Julie had requested that her father write a will. Despite feeling exhausted from lack of sleep as a consequence of the previous night's fiasco, Alice encouraged Robin to discuss the request in more detail, and was most surprised to learn that all of his children had also made the same request.

Alice wondered if now was an appropriate time to inform Robin of the missing letter to Mathew which outlined her own last will and testament. It was eating away at her, so she told him of the letter, and how someone had gained entry into the spare downstairs room, which was clearly and most definitely locked before the holiday. That same person had taken the letter addressed to Mathew, read it, kept it and acted on the contents. Now she told Robin that it was this action that had prompted Julie to suddenly, quite out of the blue, request a will be written.

Alice watched as the colour drained from her husband's face. His expression was hard for her to read. "Leave this with me," he said, "I will deal with this and get to the bottom of the whole fiasco." Alice asked for her letter to be returned to her if at all possible, for her peace of mind, which was currently in short supply. In addition, if the letter was returned it would be confirmation of the issue being raised.

This was going to be yet another sleepless night for both Robin and Alice, while their minds went into overdrive, to figure out how to handle the situation in a fair and non-judgemental manner.

True to his word, Robin dealt with the matter. The missing letter miraculously appeared on Alice's bed side table two days later. On finding the letter, Alice's heart began to race, she knew it was anxiety related, but knowing the reason didn't help her feel any easier, for she knew, this was not the end of it. The legacy of this would remain. It was like the opening of Pandora's Box.

Whoever opened Mathew's letter realised that the consequences were far reaching, as Alice was about to find out.

Much to her annoyance, Robin arranged an appointment for them to see a solicitor, to draw up a will. Alice should have been pleased, but she wasn't. Despite the fact that she herself had been encouraging Robin to write a will for many months, it had only been on the insistence of his daughter that he had finally agreed. This left Alice feeling demeaned and insignificant, as he had ignored her request and was ready to act on his daughter's instruction. The real victors were his children and they had not been punished for their actions, indeed the only consequence to their bad behaviour, was the reward of getting their own way. No one would disclose how a spare key had evolved as if by magic.

Alice chose not to pursue the matter any further. After all she had other important matters to deal with. For example, the matter of a contribution from each of them towards, their keep, just another battle to fight without the help of her husband who was too weak to stand by his wife.

Alice was at a loss as to why Robin was leaving this to her. A number of possible explanations crossed her mind. None of which made any reasonable sense. She understood what a difficult position her husband was in. He may well agree with her in principle but in practice, was it just to placate her and keep peace? Did Robin believe that as their father he should always provide for them while they continued to live in the family home? No matter how old or how much money they earned? Alice was unsure if Robin and his brothers had made any contributions to the household. Alice and her siblings had certainly been encouraged to pay their contributions and also to help with the household chores. Although this had been tough at the time, Alice later realised the important lessons learned from this.

When Alice had her first wage packet, a little brown envelope with tiny holes in and a flap to allow the money to be checked immediately on receipt, she was allowed the whole amount for herself. However, every week after that, she handed over the whole contents to her parents, which amounted to £3, 8 shillings and 11 pence. Her parents handed her the 8 shillings and 11 pence back and kept the £3 towards the household costs. She accepted this as her duty, knowing her friends were in the same situation. In many respects, although she was only fifteen years old, the fact that she was a wage earner, supporting herself, helped to reinforce her well-being and eased her transition into adulthood and the independence this brought with it. By the age of sixteen she was a strong and independent young woman. Alice pondered on this process and thought about how Robin's children would never understand this reasoning of becoming a responsible adult rather than an adolescent.

In many ways, hers and Robin's lives had been very different, therefore their values and beliefs would in some areas be in conflict, resulting in a strong difference of opinion.

Alice wasn't quite sure of Robin's true intentions with respect to his family's contribution towards the running costs of the home. But he had asked Alice to deal with it and so she would.

After a lot of deliberation, she decided the most appropriate way to address this, would be to speak to them all together at the same time. Once would be hard enough and difficult to arrange, but twice or more could be disastrous. She knew how awkward and deliberately difficult they could be at times. So timing would be paramount to the outcome.

Unfortunately, getting them all together was proving an impossible task to achieve and after failing miserably for two weeks she finally had to revoke all earlier plans and just speak with the boys together. She would speak with Julie at the earliest opportunity. The following Saturday as the boys were lounging on the sofas in their pyjamas watching television, Alice decided it was now or never. Why she was so worried and making a big deal of it was a mystery to herself. She saw this as a stepping stone for events to come. The boys would not be happy for her to disturb them from their reverie, especially as they were the worse for wear from a heavy drinking session and had not arrived home until the early hours of the morning, when once again they had arrived noisily home, arguing and swearing at each other. Someone had been sick in the downstairs toilet and Alice had found Stephen asleep on the floor in front of the fridge.

Looking through the kitchen window she saw Robin in the garden collecting dead leaves and slowly placing them in a heavy duty garden sack. He looked despondent and sad, his shoulders drooping beneath the heavy winter coat he was wearing. He had the expression of a man who preferred to be anywhere but where he currently was, which reflected her own feelings precisely.

Alice had prepared a speech in her mind of how she would approach the subject in a fair and diplomatic way, while at the same time conveying the idea, that neither their father nor she was being unreasonable. She was disappointed that Robin was not by her side, despite her telling him of her intentions, instead he had skulked off into the garden with his tail between his legs. How could he be leaving her alone to deal with this? Knowing his family well, he knew what his wife would be up against and how unpleasant things could turn out. But still he chose to stay away. Her mind wandered back to the many discussions they had about the increasing cost of living. The washing machine and tumble dryer were on day and night. The television was often left on all night long after one or another of his family had fallen asleep on the sofa. The light switch seemed to be elusive once the lights were on so consequently the electric bill was ludicrous.

With these thoughts fresh in her mind, Alice entered the lounge and with a serious note to her voice, requested for the television to be switched off, as she had something important to discuss.

"Oh here we go," said Gary. "Let's hear it." Stephen and Wayne said nothing, they did not even turn their heads towards Alice, and neither did either of them make an attempt to switch off the television. Alice had no alternative other than to walk over to the main switch and turn off the power herself. Having finally got their attention, she told them that her father and she had agreed that now they were all adults and in full time employment they should contribute a small amount towards the cost of their home, and starting from next week they would appreciate a £20 contribution. The moment Alice finished speaking she instinctively knew this would turn into the biggest argument to date. She could almost feel the tension and anger like a cloud enveloping her, she was waiting for the roar of thunder. They did not disappoint. Gary was seething with anger, his face contorted and red with rage. With deep resentment in his voice he enquired why his father had sent Alice to do his dirty work for him, or was it she who wanted their money?

"In any case," he shouted to Alice, "you will be lucky to get a penny from me." Stephen and Wayne joined in at this point saying very much the same, but this time using expletives better suited to a prison canteen than to the wife of their father. Alice attempted to calm the situation. Surely Robin could hear the commotion, why didn't he come and support her? But he remained in the garden and Alice felt very alone and defeated. She explained that it had been her intention to speak with them altogether but it had proven difficult. She asked the boys not to discuss this with their sister as she would prefer to talk with her alone.

Of course, this was extremely naive of Alice, for at his earliest opportunity, Wayne texted his sister with an exaggerated version of events, resulting in Julie arriving home like Joan of Arc ready for battle. In her defence, Julie refused to speak with Alice and insisted she only speak with her father on this matter. She scowled at Alice and with absolute venom in her voice she shouted that no way was she paying £30 a week towards the house bills and if Alice thought she would then she was living in a dream world and it was time she got used to how things would be now and in the future.

Alice looked at Julie in amazement, where on earth had that figure come from? It later transpired that Wayne had deliberately increased the amount in order to fire up Julie's temper and infuriate her so much that she would cause mayhem in the family home. The boys had conferred with one another and came to the conclusion that out of all of them, Julie was the one who could manipulate their father the most. She could turn on the tears better than any award winning actress and throw remarks at her father to make him feel guilty for marrying Alice.

Alice was surreptitiously pleased that Julie had taken on board the gauntlet, it was time Robin was involved as she herself was sick and tired of the whole fiasco and longed to escape the lot of them to live a more peaceful existence away from such selfish behaviour.

Robin came in from the garden and at his daughter's insistence, they promptly disappeared upstairs.

The boys switched the television volume to high and continued to lounge on the sofas. There was no room even had she wanted to join them. Her home was beginning to feel like a prison.

Alice needed some air, she felt overwhelmed with the recent events so she put on her winter coat and shoes and took herself off for a walk.

The days were getting shorter in theory, but to her, that day had felt like the longest day ever. Alice walked along the riverside, the bank was wet and muddy and she kicked at the stones along the path. She was deep in thought and hadn't noticed someone walking towards her.

"Hey, sis, aren't you going to say hello?" Alice looked up and saw her brother walking towards her. He was taking his dog for a walk. Darren could see at once that his sister was troubled. He did not want to pry so he suggested they meet up sometime soon for a drink together. Alice smiled, she saw right through him. "That's better Alice, a smile is much more attractive than a sad face," said Darren. She walked along with him and told him of her recent altercation with Robin's family.

He listened without interruption and when she had finished he answered her truthfully. Darren was disappointed with Robin, he should man up and deal with his family. It seemed to Darren that Robin had lost control of his family and needed to show them who the man of the house was. He also told Alice that he was worried for her health and happiness. They continued to walk for a further half hour at which point Alice kissed her brother good night. She made her way home.

No one seemed to have noticed that she had been out so long, including Robin, who was sat with the boys watching football. Feeling hungry, she went into the kitchen. Her heart sank.

The kitchen was a mess and there was no way was she going to clear up this time. It was very hard for her to ignore the mess but she did. Alice made herself some cheese and crackers and poured herself a large glass of red wine. Before climbing the stairs she called out to anyone who cared to listen, that she was having an early night. That appeared to get Robin's attention. By the time she had reached the landing he was on the stairs calling to her.

Robin followed his wife into their bedroom. He looked tired and unwell, but something else, he looked defeated. When she enquired about his conversation with Julie, Robin refused to discuss his private conversation with his daughter except to say that the matter had been dealt with.

Over the next few weeks, the atmosphere at home was so highly potent and energized, one could almost feel the sparks in the air. Although no one revisited the discussion, it was clear to see the evolving animosity. Alice began to feel uneasy and uncomfortable in her own home. When Alice came home from work and needed to relax she was unable to do so, and when Robin was on alternate week late shifts, she dreaded coming home. A home that should have been her sanctuary was gradually feeling like a prison. When alone in the house with her step children, she felt as though the house did not belong to her, despite the fact that it was her home, bought and paid for with both hers and Robin's hard earned money.

She felt out numbered. Robin and his family were enjoying the spoils of her years of hard work, they were relaxing on the furnishings she had provided and all of the luxury items she had furnished the home with. Not only had the atmosphere at home changed, she also observed a number of changes within the way Robin's family were behaving towards their father. They were behaving like comrades who had fought a battle together and come out winning. Alice knew she would never win a battle in this house, certainly not without a certain amount of strategic planning on her part. She also felt that she would always be standing alone.

Other subtle changes were also evident. Normally not affectionate with one another, their body language said otherwise. They were closing ranks. At times her step children's behaviour was childlike, the way they whispered and nudged one another when Alice entered a room. Such ridiculous playground behaviour was not lost on her; was it all part of a much bigger picture?

The most hurtful of all was her husband's behaviour. Robin began fussing and fawning around Julie, made all the worse when in public which was totally humiliating and embarrassing for Alice. This was so out of character for Robin. Other people had begun to notice and question Alice as to Robin's intentions. However, Alice suspected that he was playing a role, he had been put under a lot of pressure from his family to prove his love for them. They needed to know they were the most loved and that their father would put them first. He was playing right into their hands and putting his marriage at risk.

Unable to discuss this with her husband, Alice began to confide in her friends and seek their advice. Occasionally when Robin was on late shift she would not go home from work, instead she went to her mum's where she felt comfortable and wanted. Going back to her family home was like having a giant comfort blanket wrapped around her. One evening when Alice was feeling particularly low she sat and discussed at length how the situation at home was getting out of hand. Together they agreed what a terrible predicament Robin was in; being torn both ways.

Her mum though had only her daughter's interests at heart and could not bear to see her daughter so unhappy. She thought about the situation her daughter was in and could only compare it with her own life experience. Alice's father had been a good family man, and without a doubt had loved his wife and put her happiness above all else. With this in mind she pointed out to Alice, that one day her step children would have husbands and wives of their own, they would also have their own homes. Robin needed to put his wife first or at the very least equal to his family.

Alice began to question just how much Robin loved her. How could he allow this intolerable situation to continue? She pondered what was going on in her husband's mind, what were his real feelings? He was always so tight lipped when it came to family matters and yet was quite the opposite in regards other people's business.

His favourite saying was that he never let the right hand know what the left hand was doing.

Well he certainly didn't let Alice know what was in his mind or what plans and schemes his family were up to. What Alice knew for certain was that the whole fiasco of requesting board had been a total waste of time and energy. And if Robin had made any arrangements with them about this, he was once again keeping her out of the loop.

Alice became worn down by the whole situation and instead of long arguments when she came home from work, she took herself off upstairs to her bedroom and sat on the bed with a tray of food on her lap. There was never any room for her on the sofa and it would be a long battle to retrieve the remote control, so she preferred to read quietly in her room. At least it was clean and tidy and the en-suite was convenient, so she could stay in her room until Robin came home from work, at which point they sullenly allowed their father to watch the news.

During these times, laid on the bed, Alice let her mind wander and dream of the plans she and Robin had made for the house and the garden, the cruise they one day hoped to take and the places they planned to visit. Feeling the need to reminisce, occasionally she would seek out her old family albums and longingly stare at the photographs of her own two children when they were young, their little faces bright and alive soaking in the wonders of the many seaside resorts and foreign destinations they had visited as a family. What wonderful times they had together. Why had it all gone wrong? The childhood years were so very special. There were photographs of Mathew when he won his first football trophy and Anne Marie proudly standing by her pony clutching a very well deserved rosette.

Her tears started falling, making her eyes sting and ache. How she missed her own children, her heart ached with a deep sadness. Alice knew she was in need of a shoulder to cry on; someone who had suffered a marriage break up like herself and would understand the difficulties of a second marriage with all of the ups and downs. She had a good group of friends who she could trust, who would also understand her current situation. Maybe they could help her to put things in perspective. They regularly met at each other's homes and occasionally in a bar or restaurant.

One such meeting was arranged for the following Wednesday at Kay home.

CHAPTER FOUR

Kay lived conveniently within walking distance of her own home, which was very useful, particularly on this occasion as she intended to have a few glasses of wine.

Walking to Kay's with her bottle of Blossom Hill wine clutched tightly in her hands and a faint cool breeze blowing her hair, she felt a sense of calm and peace, a stark contrast to her clammy hands and racing heart which had been troubling her for weeks. She knew it was anxiety causing her symptoms, but tonight's peaceful feeling was a welcome change.

Most of the girls had already arrived when Alice got there and they were already drinking their first glass of wine. Kay offered Alice a glass of wine from the already opened chardonnay, which she accepted with a pained expression on her face.

"What is wrong?" enquired Kay. "I have seen that haunted look before; can we help?"

Her friends had all had their own share of grief, each one of them had been badly let down by their first husbands. They shared a common background and could relate to one another's problems. Over the years each of her friends had openly discussed their family worries and health problems. Together with an open heart and mind they approached each other's problems with sensitivity and empathy. In many ways this had helped each one of them overcome difficult periods in their lives. Just knowing that their circle of friends was available at short notice, following a text or phone call was extremely reassuring and reinforced their camaraderie.

Over the years the group of friends had increased in size, when individually they had helped other friends outside the circle and included them on their evenings out. Indeed, Alice herself had introduced two of her work colleagues to the group.

At first they would all join together for an evening out, but gradually over the years as each of the girls remarried and they were all getting older, the nights out became less frequent and the evenings spent in each other's homes more acceptable. There were nine of them in total and tonight four of them were at Kays, all willing and ready to listen to Alice's problems. Each one of them wanting to help.

Kay's little white dog jumped onto Alice's lap seeking attention and licking her arm as though he knew that she was sad. Alice stroked his curly white coat, feeling the warmth from his little body and the earthy smell from his paws. What a simple life dogs have, thought Alice, thinking about her own complicated life and how she was probably about to complicate it further.

The girls gathered around Alice, Kay sat uncomfortably on a large rocking chair. She doesn't look well, thought Alice. Kay had problems of her own. She was suffering with lower back pain and multiple joint pains, needing regular steroid injections and pain relief. She was also under a lot of pressure helping her mum and sisters to take care of her father who had a stroke only last year and was paralysed down his left side. Apparently he was now bedridden and needing daily care.

Alice wondered if now was an appropriate time to talk about her own worries, when in comparison to Kay's they probably sounded trivial and inconsequential.

However, having drunk her second glass of wine and well into the third, Alice was feeling melancholy and confused with her own feelings.

Was she being unreasonable to expect Robin's family to behave differently? Was she expecting too much from her husband?

As these thoughts whirled around her head like washing whirling around inside a washing machine, she was desperate to expel her thoughts and needed her friend's opinions, then perhaps she may feel some mental peace and even get a decent night's sleep.

Her thoughts were interrupted by the doorbell as Carol arrived with a tray of cheese and biscuits and yet another bottle of wine. Carol was the only one out of the group who wasn't divorced.

Sadly, her husband had died around the same time as Robin's first wife. Carol was step mother to his two grown up sons from his previous marriage and she also had a son and daughter of her own. In fact, all of the girls had inherited step children on their re-marriage, but none of them needed or wanted to live with their step mothers for either they owned or rented a place of their own. In this respect it was different for Alice.

They had all helped themselves to the cheese and biscuits and another glass of wine, before Alice opened up her heart to them.

They each listened and made suggestions. Helen along with her new husband owned a number of properties which they rented out. Her suggestion was for the boys to rent out one of her properties which were local, should one become available. The others agreed that this may be a good solution, enabling the boys to share the running costs and to learn to stand alone. After all, most grown men need privacy and space to entertain their girlfriends and to feel the benefits of the freedom away from the constraints of parents.

Alice knew in principle this was an excellent suggestion, but they already did as they liked and had no expenses to incur. She would need a solid reason to encourage this and also the backing of her husband. And that was likely to be the biggest obstacle.

Alice considered Helen's suggestion as she made her way home. It began to rain as she slowly made her way home, she wasn't properly dressed for the weather, and her suede court shoes began to soak up the water standing in pools on the pavement slabs. Her woollen jacket felt heavy with water and clung coldly around her. She shivered.

Her hair was hanging wet and limp about her face. Yet she had no care for how cold or wet she was. Her mind was full to bursting with sadness and torment, her evening with her friends this time had not given her much joy, but had instead given her a lot to think about.

Robin had arrived home from his evening shift and was both upset and shocked to see his wife's appearance as she entered by the back door, kicking off her sodden wet shoes. Her coat was so heavy and wet, it was impossible to hang it with the other dry ones on the coat stand, so absent-mindedly Alice hung it off the handle, knowing full well it would drip onto the door mat. She called to her husband as she made her way up the stairs to inform him that she would have a nice hot bath and go straight to bed.

He could tell she had been drinking heavily and guessed Alice had been with her friends.

Alice extravagantly poured a large amount of mineral bubble bath into the water and watched in a dream-like way as the foam rose up inside the tub. She smelled the clean fresh fragrance, like a mountain stream. Her body ached and she hoped that the bubble bath was true to the way it was advertised, but she doubted it. All the same she climbed into the warm soothing water, laid out full stretch and rested her head on the bath pillow. She lay like this for twenty minutes, all the time contemplating what Helen had said. Surely, thought Alice, the boys would be only too happy to rent a place and have their own space. Robin and she could pay the bond and the first month's rent. They could help with the furniture and soft furnishings. After all, they had more than enough furniture. In addition they still had two washing machines and a spare fridge freezer which was currently stored in the garage. The more Alice mulled this over in her mind, the more feasible it became.

Her main worry was Julie, who would no doubt miss her brothers terribly. This was something to take into consideration, although she was particularly close with Gary.

Maybe in time they could share. Alice decided she had turned it over and over in her mind enough and she would drive herself crazy if she continued like this. She removed the bath plug and laid in the bath until the water had gone, at which point she summoned the energy to climb out. Wrapping a large white fluffy bath sheet around her, Alice made her way to the bedroom. The bed looked so welcoming, but first she needed to get out her clothes for the following day and a clean uniform. Alice set the alarm for six o'clock and wearily climbed into bed.

As she closed her weary eyes she heard Robin climb the stairs.

CHAPTER FIVE

It was to be a few more weeks before Alice finally got round to discussing the idea of renting a house from Helen. For a short while the situation at home, although not improved, certainly did not get any worse. That was until the night Stephen came home early from an evening out.

Both Robin and Alice were alerted to the rushed entry through the front door. Stephen ran around the house in a blind panic closing all the curtains and switching off the lights.

He looked afraid. Robin continuously questioned Stephen as to what was happening, it was all very out of character for Stephen. He looked wild and dishevelled. Alice wondered if he was on drugs and was having some kind of paranoia attack.

Eventually, satisfied that the house was safe from whoever he expected to enter, Stephen could be heard in the kitchen pouring himself a drink. He was just about to go upstairs when the doorbell rang.

"Don't let them in, Dad, please don't open the door!" he called in blind panic.

Whoever was at the door was insistent and Alice was tempted to look through the slit in the curtain, but she restrained herself and eventually the bell ringing stopped and the door banging started. This went on for a good ten minutes. The dog next door was barking loudly. They heard the letter box rattle and the knocking stopped.

Robin called Stephen to come downstairs and explain himself.

It turned out that he was in huge debt to a local money lender to the tune of £10,000. Stephen had developed a gambling obsession and had been playing poker with the big guys.

Robin was speechless and Alice was gutted. Things were getting more complicated by the day.

Whoever was at the door had put a note through addressed to Stephen.

There was nowhere to hide. Stephen had to come clean. Hanging his head in shame he asked to speak with his father in private. Robin looked towards Alice with a look suggesting she made herself scarce. But this time she stood her ground and insisted she was staying as this was also her home and when strangers came knocking at her door in that aggressive manner, it certainly concerned her.

The letter was a demand for the money owed with interest. Threats were also made with respect to Stephens's safety. Alice did not like the sound of the threats and suggested they take the letter to the police. But Stephen was worried that would cause further animosity and he would never feel safe. He wanted the debt paying off, to put an end to it. Alice held her breath, surely Robin would not agree to give this crook all of their savings. But he did, with one condition. Stephen was to seek help with his gambling addiction.

The following day when the crook came knocking at the door, Robin handed him a check for £10000. Satisfied, he said that was the end of it and suggested he keep his son out of his way and out of the gambling clubs. Robin was glad to see the end of it. For Alice it was not the end.

Robin had given away most of their savings and she knew for sure, they would never see a penny returned to them from Stephen. Over time it would no doubt get brushed under the carpet like everything else had.

The worst of it was that Stephen showed no shame, not one ounce of remorse. Yes, he attended the first two sessions at Gamblers Anonymous, but that was intentional to appease his father. The subject was never mentioned again, even when Alice tried to return to the event, she was told that it was not up for discussion.

By Sunday of that week Robin continued his dinner time ritual of fetching his father to join them all for dinner. They called at the local pub and drank a couple of pints before returning to a freshly cooked meal, lovingly prepared by Alice.

Sometimes Alice went to collect her mum, but more often than not, her brother Darren would bring mum to his sister's house.

On most Sundays, Darren would call in to see his mum, while taking his dog for a walk. Not too far from mum's house was a small wood and open fields where Darren had spent many happy hours playing as a young boy. Alice herself had fond memories of the area. In the summer with her friends she would picnic by the small river that ran through the wood. Sometimes she took a jam jar with a makeshift string handle and a fishing net made from a bamboo cane and an old net stocking attached to the end. Very rarely did she catch the much desired stickleback, more often than not she would have a collection of water beetles and river detritus in her makeshift net.

There were many times, after her divorce, when Alice joined her brother and his dog walking around the woods following the path of the river. Darren was a good son and brother, someone Alice could always confide in. He was a good listener too and gave sound, unbiased advice.

Diane, her younger sister, had also turned to her brother when she was having a difficult time in her life. It turned out that she was a victim of domestic violence and had been concealing the fact for years. The entire family had been distraught to discover the years of mental and physical abuse she had been going through. The saving grace was that their father had not been alive to find out, so Darren and Alice had supported their sister throughout the court proceedings and subsequent divorce. Diane was now happy and remarried to a kind loving husband who was welcomed whole heartedly to the family, just as Robin had also been made welcome all those years before.

Today was one such day when Darren drove his mum to Robin and Alice's for Sunday dinner.

She was relieved about this as once again Alice had not slept well and was already weary from the preparation of dinner and the pile of laundry she had already done. The weather did not look very promising in terms of drying the washing, but she decided to risk it, as one way or another it needed to be dry so she could iron it that evening. Working long hours, she had to plan ahead in terms of meal preparation and household tasks, otherwise the jobs would pile up at the weekend.

During the meal both Robin's Dad and Alice's mum observed for themselves how the atmosphere was beginning to get worse, the children seemed to have little respect for their father and step mum. The situation wasn't helped by the fact that the much needed repair work on the house was not progressing. The lounge carpet was getting increasingly dirty as a consequence of the hallway floor being exposed down to the foundations which Alice thought was a health and safety issue. Especially as her mum and father in law were elderly and already unsteady on their feet. They could quite easily trip themselves up while negotiating between the joists.

The damp paintwork in the hallway was showing signs of black mould. The original plans to redecorate the lounge were on hold until the insurance company had decided how to proceed.

Neither Robin or Alice were satisfied with the way the insurance company had handled the claim, resulting in Alice complaining to the company on more than one occasion and eventually contacting the ombudsman.

Recently she had noticed her father in law coughing a lot more and wondered if the damp was bothering him. She was concerned for his health; he was always a heavy smoker and she also noticed he was getting increasingly short of breath and had an expiratory wheeze. Even on the flat over a short distance she observed him struggling. She also observed he was helping himself to less and less food and struggled with the small portions on his plate.

Alice understood it must be a struggle for him to eat, being so breathless. Alice's mum had also noticed and during the journey home they spoke about what a decent man Robin's father was. Later in the evening Alice voiced her concerns to Robin about his father's failing health. She had a good idea what the problem may be. After all, she had nursed enough patients with lung disease to know the signs and symptoms. Alice was sensitive in her approach to Robin, she did not wish to worry her husband or cause him alarm.

He enquired of his wife what he could do to help his father. He was a proud man and likely would not admit to feeling unwell, he would not want to be a burden to his sons.

Alice suggested that she speak to his father. He may feel more comfortable speaking to herself with her medical knowledge and skills. Robin thought that was an excellent idea. So the following day on her way home from work, she called in to see her father in law and persuaded him to attend his GP practice for an elderly health review. Alice arranged the appointment for two days' time. Robin's father was more than happy for Alice to take him.

On the morning of the appointment Alice drove her father in law to the surgery and with his permission she accompanied him to the consulting room.

Due to his deterioration of hearing, Robin's father requested for Alice to explain to the GP what was bothering him. Young Dr Fitzwilliam was extremely kind and empathetic in his approach.

After a series of questions related to past medical history, previous occupational history, a chest examination and a spirometry lung function test, the doctor came to a decision. Dr Fitzwilliam Wrote a prescription for prednisolone steroid tablets, antibiotics and a Ventolin inhaler to reduce his chest tightness and relax his airways.

Arrangements were made for a chest x-ray and a follow up appointment.

On the journey home Alice spoke about how the steroids should help to reduce inflammation and the antibiotics with any underlying infection. Before leaving the house Alice demonstrated how the inhaler was to be used. She hated leaving him alone in his home and felt so sorry for him.

Alice decided that Robin and his brothers needed encouragement to visit every day. Thankfully they all agreed on this, therefore every evening after work, one of the brothers would visit their father and every weekend he continued to have his Sunday meal with Robin and Alice. In addition to these arrangements, Alice routinely cooked an extra dinner for her father in law and Robin would take it to the house. Alice guessed that one plated meal was likely to last 2 days as he was struggling to eat very much. But she wanted to make sure that he had a good nutritious meal at least 4 times a week. Alice also called in on her way home from work. It was on one of these visits she noticed how much her father in law was deteriorating. He looked afraid and frail, this distressed Alice deeply. She suggested to Robin that his father came to stay with them for a while until he improved. But in her heart and with her medical experience she felt sure that this was unlikely.

Alice prepared herself for another of Robin's family moving in with them. In her heart she knew it was the right thing to do for her father in law. She could see he was weak and unwell and in need of tender loving care. Robin's father took no persuading; he had resigned himself to being cared for by his family. This must have been difficult for such a proud man who, until recently, had been strong and helpful to his children and grandchildren.

The downstairs room was prepared for him. The two divan beds were packed away into the garage and a new divan bed purchased which could be raised at the head and foot of the bed. A bedside table was put close to the bed with a reading lamp. A small chest of drawers was emptied and made ready for his clothes and clean linen for the bed. A television was placed on the chest which had been positioned at the foot of the bed. The room was bright and cheerful with two large windows. The blinds had blackouts behind them to prevent too much light at night. Alice made up the bed with fresh linen and collected extra pillows to support his neck and shoulders. The room was ready.

The house was busier than ever with even more washing and ironing. However, her father in law was no trouble and was so humble and grateful for the care he received. It was good for him to be surrounded by his family, including his grandchildren, who he loved whole heartedly. Robin and Alice reminded them to be especially quiet when they came home in the evening so as not to disturb their grandfather. However there were times when this request was forgotten, and Alice became concerned at the increased frequency of her father in law's restless nights, rendering him exhausted the following day. From time to time Robin's brothers came to visit their father and with Robin they sat together in the garden or the conservatory and reminisced about their own young lives. They looked at old family photographs and talked about their mum. It was poignant to see them all together united in their love.

Alice also enjoyed spending time chatting to her father in law. Both keen gardeners, they spent hours discussing growing methods and which varieties of tomatoes and potatoes to grow.

Usually they sat comfortably in the conservatory overlooking the garden, enjoying the views.

But these occasions were getting less and less as his health deteriorated, until eventually, getting out of bed was a struggle.

Alice herself began to feel the strain of working and running a home for seven people. Most evenings she would not get the opportunity to relax until well after ten in the evening. Robin's children continued to be troublesome with each other and antagonistic towards herself. She had hoped they would help a little with their grandfather, but this was not the case. She was disappointed about the little time they spent with him, despite knowing of his serious health.

Then one evening a phone call from Helen gave her a glimmer of hope. At the end of the month one of her rented properties would be available. It was a three-bedroom semi-detached house with a small garden. The house was local and Alice knew the area well. The rent was reasonable and the boys would have no trouble sharing the cost.

She breathed a great sigh of relief. Alice thanked her friend and said she would be in touch.

Timing was important when speaking to Robin about his family, something she had learned over the years having made a number of mistakes. Discussing important issues when he wasn't in the right frame of mind was pointless as he was not receptive. However, this was too important to put off. A delay could mean a lost opportunity.

When Robin came in from work, Alice tried to determine his mood and frame of mind; she did not want to get this wrong. His father was asleep and the family had all gone out to a night club, she guessed they would be late home. She prepared Robin a light meal of chicken salad with new potatoes and poured him a large glass of wine. She poured herself one and joined him in the lounge to watch the news.

"I've got some news," said Alice and she told him of her phone call from Helen. She asked Robin to approach the boys and inform them of the house and she suggested together they could help out with the bond and the first month's rent. Alice got a little enthusiastic about which pieces of furniture they could have, and how she would sort bedding and towels for them. Robin listened without interruption.

Once again he declined the task of talking with them. It was as if he was afraid of his own children. Alice began to feel impatient and although patience is a virtue, hers was fast running out. Alice lost her temper with Robin for the first time in their marriage. She demanded an explanation. Feeling totally worn out and at the end of her tether, Alice began to cry.

Tears did not normally come easy to her but the months of pent up emotion finally spilled over, releasing the tension she had been carrying with her for months.

Robin explained that he did not want to drive a wedge between himself and his children. He believed they were so stubborn that any damage would be irreparable. Now Alice knew why her husband constantly let her down. She also understood why he had become over affectionate with his daughter. She was furious and enquired what about the wedge he was putting between them and was he aware of the danger of driving her away and putting his marriage at risk?

Alice felt that she could no longer compete with his family and neither should she. Alice reminded her husband of the conversation on their fifth wedding anniversary. It was now approaching their sixth.

Upset and deflated she went to bed leaving Robin in front of the television where he remained until the early hours of the morning, when he was disturbed by his family returning in a state of drunkenness. She felt her husband slide in the bed beside her and turn away from her.

The next day, tired from yet another bad night, Alice decided to speak to the boys herself, after all, she had nothing to lose. It was a long day at work for her.

Thursday was her longest day, doing a nine-hour shift to cover late clinics. It had been at her own suggestion that the surgery had at least two late surgeries to enable full time workers the accessibility of the service after normal working hours. It had turned out to be very successful. She appreciated how difficult it could be for working people to visit the surgery or to bring elderly relatives who relied on their working family to transport them to the surgery.

It was getting dark as she drove along the winding lanes which for most part had no lighting.

Alice had driven this same route every day to work and knew every twist and turn, but on this occasion, her mind was wandering and she was planning how to approach the tetchy subject of the available house. Suddenly head lights were dazzling her eyes and the loud beep of a car horn dragged her thoughts back to her task in hand. She had unwittingly crossed the central line and was drifting into the oncoming traffic. Quickly she pulled the car over, missing a head on collision by a fraction of a second. Alice was visibly shaken and ashamed of herself for her lack of concentration. Yes, she was also tired but this was no excuse. Her mind was too preoccupied with her personal circumstances. Something had to change and soon.

At home everyone was sat in the lounge watching the television. She could smell the casserole cooking which she had prepared before leaving for work. Robin had put a light under the vegetables prepared that morning which were to accompany the casserole. After checking that the food was satisfactory, Alice called 'hi' to everyone as she entered the lounge, but no one answered except her husband. He offered to make her a cup of tea. She gratefully accepted. Still feeling in shock from the near miss of a serious accident, Alice was not really in the mood for talking, so was happy sitting quietly while the family lay around listening to the latest *Top of the Pops*. She had long ago lost track of who was in the charts although it seemed only a short time ago she was dancing with Robin in the local night club. Where does time go, she thought? Alice looked at Gary. At his age she was married with her first child. By all accounts she felt that she had behaved in a much more mature manner than any of Robin's family. In fact, she was more grown up at sixteen than they were in their twenties.

Robin came in with the tea and suggested she rest while he plated the dinners. For once there was no arguing, everyone seemed to be enjoying the same programme. This was a rare occurrence and one that Alice savoured. She enquired about her father in law. Eventually, Julie answered that he was resting in his room.

Thinking her father in law might appreciate some company, Alice popped her head around his door. She could hear his laboured breathing and saw the duvet on the bed rising and falling with each respiration. He didn't look comfortable and was too far down the bed off his pillows. This was not helping with his breathing. He needed to be lifted up the bed to enable his poorly functioning lungs a chance of better expansion. If she had lifted him alone it may have been uncomfortable on his back, so Alice called for assistance from Robin. He called back saying he was just taking the dinners into the lounge as they were eating off trays. So Robin took four trays into the lounge so as not to disturb his family viewing the television. He then came and assisted Alice with his father. Very gently they lifted him up the bed. This, of course, woke him up. He thanked them both for their help. Robin offered to bring his father a small meal on a tray, but he declined and said that maybe later a cup of tea and a couple of ginger biscuits would be just fine. They looked at one another then. No words needed to be spoken. They each knew what the other was thinking.

Alice did not have much appetite either. She picked at her meal and left most of it. Everyone else appeared to have enjoyed the meal very much which pleased her. Together, Robin and Alice cleared away the dirty dishes, filled the dishwasher and sat down with a glass of wine. It was getting late, yet she still needed to prepare for the following day's meal. Fortunately, there was a home-made steak pie in the freezer that she had made a few weeks earlier. Alice tended to make food dishes in double the quantity, allowing her to freeze one for another time. She took the pie out to defrost and checked they had some frozen chips and peas. This done, Alice returned to the lounge and to her glass of wine. Robin poured more wine into her glass and she didn't stop him.

Everyone was still in the lounge, so Alice decided it was a good opportunity to mention Helen's rental property.

During the advertisement break she told the boys about the availability of the house and how it would be perfect for them to share. They all stared at her, open mouthed as though she had just asked them play on a motorway. Gary became aggressive in his manner and swore at Alice for daring to bring the subject up. Stephen was just as bad and said with his circumstances, no way was he able to use his wages to pay rent and other costs. Wayne, although less aggressive, said he also was not interested. The time was not right for him.

Alice was not expecting them to welcome the news with open arms. Fundamentally she was not at all surprised. Throughout the conversation Julie was heaving and sighing and looking at her father for some kind of retaliation against his wife. She was bitterly disappointed that her father made no attempt to become involved in the conversation. Julie was not the only one disappointed.

As it turned out, it was a blessing in disguise that the boys did not rent the house.

Exactly one week later, Alice received a very distressing phone call from her daughter, Anne Marie, who was distraught and so tearful it took her mum some time before she could comprehend what Anne Marie was trying to say. Eventually after listening to the soothing words from her mum, Anne Marie explained. It transpired that as usual she had spent the weekend away with her fiancé Andrew in East Sussex. Unfortunately, Andrew had needed to move south to find employment in his chosen career. He had studied politics for many years and the career opportunities in the Midlands were not good at the time and he had great aspirations Therefore it was a sacrifice to leave behind Anne Marie but they both had known it was for the greater good. In time they hoped to come to a compromise with respect to their chosen careers and find a location to put down new roots. Meanwhile, Anne Marie was thoroughly enjoying her work as a landscape gardener and horticulturist. She also had studied hard for many years in addition to her voluntary work with the local wild life trust.

Until recently, she had grown much attached to her home. It had been a struggle for her to save the deposit for her first mortgage and Anne Marie needed to make many sacrifices. However, it all seemed worth the effort when she finally purchased a small two-bedroom cottage on the outskirts of the city. The cottage was everything Anne Marie had dreamed of. But tonight those dreams had been shattered. It was dark when Anne Marie arrived home to a cold empty house. Since Andrew had moved south, her home felt so lonely. Although she had lived in the cottage for two years before Andrew moved in, she had grown accustomed to sharing her home and it had been especially comforting in the evening to return home to a warm home and loving arms.

She longed for the day when they would be sharing a home again. A home they would buy as a couple. As she walked up the poorly lit path leading to her home it occurred to her that the path was unusually wet considering it had been a dry evening. At the time she hadn't concerned herself too much with the thought. Her train journey had been long, with many changes on the route. Some parts of the journey were most uncomfortable, especially on the cross country train which was packed and for most of the journey she was sat on her upturned suitcase near the luggage compartment. A hot drink and a good night's sleep were her only thoughts.

Putting her small suitcase in the hallway, she collected the post and placed it on the pine table they had lovingly restored together when Andrew had first moved in. She filled the kettle, collected her favourite china mug with the little pony painted on the side, a reminder of her childhood passion for horse riding. Then she glanced down at her mail. Her attention was immediately drawn to an envelope with police emblazoned across the top in large yellow and black writing. With trembling hands, she opened the envelope. The message inside informed Anne Marie that her outbuilding had been set on fire by arsonists while she was away. The whole building had exploded like a fire bomb, due to the volatile contents inside. She had her petrol mower in there with a spare can of fuel. In addition, there had been at least four cans of paint, paint stripper and turpentine. The neighbours had called out the emergency services, and quite rightly so. The fire department had contained the inferno, but nothing was saved and her whole garden was burnt to the ground. The lawn, all the borders and her container pots were either melted or cracked. Fortunately, the garden was surrounded by an ancient old wall on two sides, but the fence border had been burnt to cinders.

When she went outside and checked the damage she only had a small torch. Even with the lounge and kitchen lights on it was difficulty to get a full picture. The little she did manage to see was heart breaking. The outbuilding was no more than a charcoal mess. Nothing remained except evidence of burnt out metal which were the remains of hers and Andrew's bikes. The tools, the lawnmower, strimmer and all of her DIY equipment had been burnt to cinders.

Alice was speechless as Anne Marie with a trembling voice informed her mum of the disaster that she had arrived home to. Without any hesitation, Alice said she was on her way. The journey took Alice around forty minutes but it felt much longer. She didn't enjoy driving at night, even in good weather conditions and after only fifteen minutes of driving it began to rain, resulting in glare off the headlights on the dark shiny tarmac. Most of the journey was through twisting lanes. Alice needed to really concentrate when oncoming traffic didn't dip their lights.

She could feel her head tightening up and a sickly pain moving across her forehead. It was a combination of stress, worry and poor driving conditions.

The lane immediately leading to Anne Marie's house was not accessible to traffic so Alice parked her car on the main road close to where the lane led off. It worried her leaving the car there overnight knowing the hooligans who had set fire to Anne Marie's property could just as well do damage to her own car. Brushing this thought aside, she walked down the little lane. There was one street light at the end of the lane, a sodium light and it threw very little light out. The light did create eerie shadows so Alice felt relieved when she finally opened the wooden gate leading up a pretty path to the front door. Alice didn't need to see the damage, she could smell the smoke and the incinerated ruin of her daughter's property. The rain which was now falling heavy was evidently dampening down the remainder of the hot debris and ash.

She had her own key to the house and Anne Marie was expecting her, so she let herself in, calling out to her daughter as she entered the hallway.

"I'm here, Mum, in the kitchen," called out Anne Marie. Alice kicked off her wet shoes and hung her coat on the hall stand, her daughter was in the kitchen cooking soup and apologised to her mum for not having any fresh milk or bread as the shops were already closed when she arrived home. Alice had anticipated this and produced a bag full of shopping which she had gathered from her own cupboards on the way out. Alice had bread, butter, cheese, fruit, crackers, wine and milk. Thinking only of her daughter, she suggested that Anne Marie have a nice soak in the bath after they had eaten the soup and then they could open the wine, watch a film and then survey the damage properly in the morning. While her daughter was in the bath, Alice rang Robin and explained what had happened. She told him of her plans to stay the night.

The following day Monday, Alice was on a late shift. Anne Marie rang work and explained her situation at home. Her boss was very understanding and said she was to take off as much time as needed, to secure the safety of her home. Alice needed to be at work for one thirty so she was up early along with her daughter. With trepidation they went through the back door to see the horror before them. It was unbelievable, even worse than either of them had anticipated. The whole garden looked as though a nuclear bomb had landed and burnt away all sign of life.

What they hadn't bargained for was the damage to the house. Although the outbuilding was at least eighteen feet away from the property, the intense heat had cracked her lounge, kitchen and bathroom windows and the PVC frames and sills had melted. The back door had also areas of damage and the roof guttering was damaged, probably from the flames shooting up and giving off sparks. It was going to be a big clean up job. Anne Marie needed help. Alice rang the surgery and briefly explained the situation. She requested a day's leave for the following day. She was granted the leave, therefore enabling plans to be made in terms of arranging for a skip to shovel all of the debris into. Anne Marie contacted the police on the number quoted on the letter. They gave her a crime number for insurance purposes and said they were sending a police officer to interview her. Anne Marie arranged for a medium skip to be delivered the following morning.

Around mid-morning an elderly police officer called in to see Anne Marie. He was extremely sympathetic and helpful. He told them both how it saddened him that a nice young woman had been targeted in this way. He had daughters of his own, so he felt their pain and distress. He gave Anne Marie safety advice with respect to potential further trouble and informed them that the local police suspected a group of young men who had recently moved into the area and were already known to them. However, they had no proof.

Unfortunately, Alice had to leave her daughter for the time being, with the promise of driving back that evening and staying over once again so that her daughter was not alone in the house overnight. She arrived home with just enough time to grab her uniform and prepare a packed lunch. Robin was not at home; he had already left for work. The house was quiet; Robin's family were still in bed. Before leaving, she popped her head around the door of her father in law's bedroom. Even though it was midday he was sound asleep. She hoped his grandchildren would take care of him until Robin arrived home. He was due home mid-afternoon.

Alice left Robin a note explaining her plans to return to her daughter's home straight from work that evening and she packed an overnight bag, including an old jumper and trousers. She found her wellingtons that were in the under stairs cupboard, a waterproof coat and leather gloves. She had a lot of work to do the following day.

Throughout her working day, she felt distracted. She knew it was important to concentrate on her work, for it was imperative that she did not make any mistakes. In her break, she rang her daughter to remind her to be vigilant at all times. Alice still felt very uneasy about the situation; she was feeling a rising panic within her body and impending danger for her daughter.

The afternoon clinic was hectic. Today was the routine baby vaccination clinic. Alice enjoyed meeting the new parents when they came with their eight week old infants for their first vaccinations of their primary course. She adored their chubby little arms and legs and hated hearing then cry as she gave the vaccinations. Although the procedure was distressing for both parent and baby, Alice knew it was for their long term protection and this is what she conveyed to the anxious parents when their babies screamed loudly until their little faces were scarlet.

The worry for your children never goes away, thought Alice. She thought about the words her mum often repeated. "They make your arms ache as babies and heart ache as adults." How very true, thought Alice.

It was nine thirty when she finally sat down with her daughter. Anne Marie had made her mum a light supper and opened a bottle of wine. They talked through the day's events and settled for an early night.

The skip arrived on time. They had been up since seven, shovelling the debris into manageable piles. The galvanized steel wheelbarrow which had been left at the top of the garden, was still intact, which was very fortunate as they filled it up repeatedly over the next five hours until, exhausted, they stopped for a break. The wooden picnic bench had been burnt to a cinder and the garden chairs had melted into a sticky glutinous mess. So although they were both extremely filthy, covered in soot and ash, they returned to the kitchen to have a well-earned rest. The problem was how to feel once again enthusiastic enough to complete the task. Anne Marie tuned the radio in to Smooth FM, she knew it was her mum's favourite station and sure enough two coffees and a full packet of biscuits later they were up and at it, until the job was complete.

Anne Marie surveyed the remnants of her garden. The lawn and vegetable patch were gone along with her outbuilding. Suddenly, Anne Marie did not want to be there. She felt like running away and leaving everything behind. If only Andrew had been with her, he could have held her in his arms and comforted her like only a lover can. Her mum had hugged her many times over the past two days, and that was nice, however it was Andrew she craved.

It was dusk when they finished. Their backs and shoulders were stiff and sore. They both needed a good long soak and most definitely a scrub. Alice told her daughter to have the first bath, as she needed to prepare her things, for she was returning to work the next day. Alice was also at work the following day and needed to be up very early for the extra distance she needed to travel.

No doubt the roads would be extremely busy for the morning commute and no way was she going to keep the patients waiting for their appointment slot.

Andrew rang while her daughter was in the bath. She filled him in on the day's events and how together they had filled a skip with tons of burnt out debris. She told Andrew that she was trying to keep her daughter's spirits up and yet she felt helpless in many ways. Andrew asked Alice to encourage Anne Marie to visit him at the weekend and not to fret about any more work on the garden as he was planning to visit in two weeks and Anne Marie was to have a rest. Anne Marie called downstairs to her mum requesting that she bring the phone to her in the bathroom; Alice did as she was bid.

That night she could not find sleep, her mind was tormented with many questions. Amongst them was the reason as to why neither Anne Marie's father nor brother had offered to help, not even for a few hours. Although only a couple of hours' drive away. In addition, her stepfather and three step brothers who were only forty minutes away didn't bother to help either. They had been left to struggle alone. Alice was not happy.

CHAPTER SIX

The following morning both Alice and her daughter left early for work. It was a long day for Alice, she could not get her daughter out of her mind. And this was compounded by her own situation at home. As the day wore on she was feeling the effects of the constant shovelling, bending and lifting. Why? thought Alice, why would anyone deliberately set fire to her daughter's property in such mindless delinquent behaviour? If the police were right about their suspects, it begged the question what are the parents doing while their offspring are deliberately and systematically causing grief to others.

Her thoughts were interrupted when Dr Cosgrove requested her assistance with a wound that needed dressing. It turned out to be an extensive procedure. The patient already had one below the knee amputation, as a result of damaged veins from drug use. And now the other leg was in a terrible condition and required a Doppler assessment, washing, cleansing and a number of dressings and layers of bandages. It was a long and painful procedure for the patient and Alice had so much empathy for the young woman whose records showed that she had suffered a tragic life which had led her into the life she was now leading.

Somehow it put things momentary into perspective and she didn't mind, not one little bit, that she would be late home after clearing away the soiled dressings and washing down the clinical area.

Robin was sat at the kitchen table when she arrived home. He noticed how exhausted his wife looked and decided a cup of tea was out of the question. He poured her a large glass of wine.

He enquired after Anne Marie. Alice filled him in on the details the best she could, but never said a word about the useless men in her life who could have, should have, but didn't bother to offer assistance.

The house was unusually quiet; she could hear the news reader on the television discussing the recent political situation. Alice guessed that her father in law was most likely in the lounge making the most of being able to watch something of his choice. Alice thought that the rest of the family must be out; otherwise a cartoon or a teenage sit-com would be on. Sitting opposite her father in law she noticed how much weight he had lost recently and his breathing was getting more difficult. She guessed that his lungs were getting more diseased and obstructed and likely another course of steroids and antibiotics would be needed before the week was out.

They sat talking about the events on the news and how the world was changing. He got most of his pleasure from reminiscing about his past. Alice considered her own autumn years. Would she look back and only remember all that was good? She truly hoped that would be the case.

Robin called to Alice to help him plate the meals out. "Where is everyone?" Alice enquired. She had noticed seven plates laid on the counter.

"Oh, they have gone to a theme park for the day," sighed Robin. "But I must have a meal ready for them to warm up when they come home." What? thought Alice, she guessed that they would be stuffing themselves with burgers, chips and lashings of alcohol all day but she said nothing.

Sure enough, at one o'clock in the morning a noisy bunch of adolescents came home and tumbled into their beds. Robin rolled over in bed towards Alice and whispered that they would probably eat the dinner for breakfast. But she knew for certain they would not be out of bed, anytime resembling breakfast. Closer to the truth would be dinner.

In the early hours of the morning, Alice went downstairs to check on her father in law who was coughing loudly and disturbed her sleep. No one else appeared concerned. She called to let him know that she was entering his bedroom. He was distressed and struggling to breathe. She helped him up the bed and supported him with extra pillows. She then set up a nebulizer device with the prescribed medication of salbutamol and placed the mask over his mouth. As the salbutamol infused, moist air penetrated his airways and she could almost see the fear leaving his frightened face. She made a mug of tea for them both and sat with him until he had finished his tea and drifted off to sleep.

By this time, Robin was up for his early shift. He was surprised to see his wife up before himself and suggested she take the day off work. Alice would hear nothing of the sort. She had never taken a day off work unless she was genuinely ill and she saw no reason to change her values now. There was no point going back to bed, so she sat with Robin a while, made him a packed lunch and kissed him goodbye. With two hours to spare before she needed to leave for work, she tidied the house, emptied the bins, put a load of washing on and prepared a chicken casserole for the evening meal. Robin planned to be home around two o'clock to be with his father.

In her lunch break, Alice contacted Mathew. He apologised for not being able to support his sister but thought others may have helped. When Alice explained that no one but herself had been there for Anne Marie, Mathew was even more upset. He had always been such a good, loyal brother. They had been very close in their younger days and Mathew had always been very supportive on a social and financial level. He said he felt ashamed that their father had not attempted to help his daughter and he would surely be having words with him. His mum warned him against this course of action, advising that it would only result in more hard feelings. After speaking with Mathew, Alice rang Anne Marie who was in a more positive frame of mind considering what had recently occurred. The planned arrival of Andrew at the weekend had given her a positive focus.

Hearing that her daughter was coping well helped lift her own mood and the knowledge that she would not be alone in the house at the weekend gave Alice some comfort.

Alice also had something special to look forward to that weekend. Her Christmas gift from Robin was two tickets to see a Rod Stewart concert at Birmingham NEC, something she had been wishing to do for many years. Just thinking about the evening made her smile.

They had an amazing night and she felt a million dollars in her navy Betty Jackson dress and Faith shoes. Robin looked fabulous and her heart flipped as she put her arm through his.

As Rod Stewart sang all the old familiar songs and some new, she felt all of her cares drift away. She was transported for a short while to being the happy carefree girl she once was.

Still feeling the joy from her night out with Robin, Alice coped well with the usual Sunday dinner fiasco followed by television tantrums. The weekend once again over, she was ready to face another week.

Monday morning, Anne Marie phoned her mum early, knowing she would be leaving for work.

She told her mum, that Andrew and she had a nice relaxing weekend together, everything was going well until it was time for Andrew to leave. When Anne Marie walked him to his car she had noticed a group of young men run off. They had broken his windscreen and snapped off the wing mirrors. Andrew was unable to drive back south until the emergency windscreen repair team came and repaired his car. It had been late when Andrew had finally arrived home, Anne Marie had worried about him the entire night. She had once again reported the crime to the police, who said they would provide a crime number for the insurance. Andrew had driven back full of worry for the safety of his fiancé.

If Alice had thought that this was the worst it was going to get for her daughter, she could not have been more mistaken. Friday evening of the same week, she received a further phone call from Anne Marie. At first it was difficult to comprehend what her distraught daughter was trying to say, and when Alice finally understood what had occurred she told her daughter that she was coming over immediately. Alice grabbed her car keys.

Robin had only ten minutes earlier left the house to fetch some bread, as for some reason an unusually large amount had been consumed during the day.

She wrote a quick note for Robin and told her father in law that she would be in touch.

Alice once again drove to her daughter's home, more or less on auto-pilot. For the whole journey, her mind was going into overdrive, her imagination running wild. A hatred against the culprits was building up inside her, akin to a volcano about to erupt. She could put no faces to the culprits, who were no doubt the same group of hooligans that had been terrorizing her daughter for weeks. Hate was an unfamiliar emotion to her. Alice was generally consumed with love. She believed that love and kindness were essential for wellbeing and yet somehow, the emotion of hate had crept inside her psyche. No doubt Sigmund Freud would not be at all surprised in her ability to feel such hatred. But it was not a good feeling, in truth the emotion was draining and sapping the love away from her heart.

Fortunately, the roads were clear and her journey uneventful.

Feeling a knot in her stomach as she walked along the dark isolated path that lead to her daughter's lovely cottage, Alice began to feel nauseous. She would not allow her daughter to witness her own distress as Alice needed to keep a clear head in order to be of most help.

Once again as she neared the house, the smell of a recent fire engulfed the air. The garden gate was still smouldering and the front garden scorched but that was nothing compared to the damage to the front door. The pretty bay window had numerous breaks and cracks in the glass, but not from fire damage. More likely due to missiles deliberately thrown at the window for maximum effect...

Fear rising up inside her caused Alice to retch, she was finding it difficult not to vomit as the entered through the badly damaged front door. Inside the hall, the carpet was badly burnt and a broken glass bottle was on its side on the floor.

Anne Marie was sat on the sofa, holding her head in her hands.

"Why, Mum, why?" she sobbed and sobbed, her whole body shaking with shock. Alice sat with her on the sofa and tried to sooth her daughter, to no avail. She wrapped her arms around her daughter and rocked her gently. No words were spoken, no words were needed.

Eventually she made them both chamomile tea, which they quietly sipped together while awaiting the police. Once again the neighbours had rung the fire service who had responded quickly enough to prevent further spread of fire through the property. The main fire damage was to the hallway, however the smoke had penetrated up the stairs and into the lounge. The whole house smelled of smoke.

Once again, a police officer was dispatched to take a statement from Anne Marie. He informed them that a fire safety team were on the way to put metal shutters up to the doors and windows.

In effect, the house was being fire proofed against further damage.

Within an hour of the policeman leaving. A team of men came and sealed up the cottage with steel shutters. The fire safety officer sat down with Anne Marie and her mum and explained that it appeared a home-made petrol bomb had been shoved through the letter box and a further one thrown on the garden. He advised Anne Marie to collect her belongings and go to a place of safety. The back door was made assessable and Anne Marie was provided with a padlock so that only she had access.

The police had informed them that she was now the target of the local gang who were terrorising young women at random. They had now moved up to a new level of terror, and the police were taking this as a very serious incident.

Reluctant to leave her home, Alice gently encouraged her daughter to collect a few belongings and come back home with her. She reminded her daughter that her home was for her family as well as Robin's and that would never change.

Anne Marie protested that she would not be happy living with Robin's family and besides how would she commute to the city in time for work? But there really was only one solution and so Anne Marie agreed to go back with her mum.

Together they gathered essentials including her passport and all legal documentation. In addition, all of her jewellery and items of value were packed up. Anne Marie packed a number of suitcases and two boxes of sentimental goods such as photo albums, picture frames and ornaments. It was past eleven in the evening when the car was packed full of her daughter's possessions…

It was nearly midnight when they finally arrived at what Alice considered her family home.

Robin and his family were all sprawled across the sofas in the lounge watching the television. They had all been drinking as the number of empty cans on the coffee table suggested.

Other than Robin, no one sat up to make room for their obviously distraught step sister and step mum. Robin fetched a drink for them both and listened to the events that had occurred. He said of course Anne Marie could move in.

At the mention of moving in, Robin's family soon became interested in the conversation.

"So which room are you planning to have?" said Julie. The boys all looked at one another.

"Well there is no room with us," said Stephen. "You will have to share with Julie because Granddad is in the downstairs room." Julie was not impressed and stomped up the stairs.

She slammed the bedroom door hard.

By this time, Anne Marie could take no more. She said she would sleep on the sofa, if someone would vacate it long enough for her to get her head down.

Alice, already fraught and close to breaking point, was fed up of being the dutiful wife, step mum and daughter in law. Something inside her had been broken. She snapped and the words that came from her mouth, were so alien to her that she almost felt as though someone was pulling her strings. "That is it. I have had my fill of the lot of you. This is my house and this is my daughter. She is just as entitled to be here as the rest of you. But I tell you all now. I am moving out, taking all of my furniture and belongings. Anne Marie is coming with me.

"She is my priority and I will not see her sleeping on a sofa while you have the luxury of your own rooms in my house. You live rent free, board free and give nothing in return. My daughter has been to hell and back, worked hard to provide herself with a home and gone without the things you all take for granted. We will be gone tomorrow."

Anne Marie began to sob. "Please, Mum, you don't have to do this." Alice looked towards Robin who had not spoken one word. He looked utterly defeated.

"Yes I do," she answered. "My husband needs to take control of his family, it will be easier with me away, and I am desperately in need of a calm retreat. Robin knows I love him that will not change. I am changing address on a temporary basis until you are safe, happy and settled. It is the very least I can do as your own father is a waste of space. You and I will enjoy some long overdue mother and daughter time.

"When you move down south to be with Andrew, I don't doubt that with your busy work schedule it will be difficult for you to visit me very often. I love you Anne Marie, let me do this for you. Your need is greater than Robin's. He will get his brothers on board to help with his father or even, dare I say it, his own children?"

Too exhausted to argue, Anne Marie said nothing. Robin and his family skulked off to bed, while Alice gathered bedding for the sofa.

The following morning, Alice rang her friend Helen to enquire if the house was still available to rent. Apparently it was, and much to Helen's surprise, Alice agreed on a six-month contract for herself and Anne Marie. She briefly told her friend of the situation at home and the terrible situation her daughter was in... Helen told Alice she could collect the keys whenever was convenient. Anne Marie's belongings were still in the car which was parked in the staff car park. This did not escape the attention of her work colleagues, naturally they were inquisitive especially when the nurse's car was packed with boxes and suitcases. They were already aware of the first incident at her daughter's home and were all saddened to hear of the further arson attack. When Alice requested two days' annual leave to help her daughter move out, the practice manager did not hesitate in saying yes. Later in the day she provided the manager with her new address and personal bank account details. Instead of paying her wages into the joint account, she now needed every penny to pay for the rent and utilities over the next few months. She felt a faint pang of bitterness at the idea of the financial situation she was getting herself into. Robin and his family were all living in her mortgage free home, with all of the comforts and utilities.

Yet she and Anne Marie were soon to be living in rented accommodation. How can this be fair? thought Alice, why am I moving out, why, after all my daughter has been through?

Alice worried that her daughter might carry the burden of her decision to leave Robin and blame herself should the future be difficult for her mum. So Alice reassured Anne Marie that she had not been the catalyst, not even the spark, only an opportunity to help her onto a different path.

Deep down inside, she knew why she was moving out, it was for Anne Marie. But also she wanted to remind Robin and his family what a strong, determined woman she was and perhaps by moving out it would hopefully be the wakeup call her husband needed, in order to help his grown up family become mature responsible adults. Even while she was thinking about this, Alice had her doubts. She hoped she was wrong. In her mind's eye, was the fantasy of his family all happy and settled in their own place. Alice would be more than happy to help them in every possible way. She envisaged a time when she could return from work and find her home still clean and tidy as she had left it. A time when she would be able to relax and watch the television without arguments and enjoy a peaceful meal. Her thoughts went into overdrive as she imagined how much easier her life would be with less laundry and cooking. The extra money would come in handy also. They could perhaps afford to go on the long awaited cruise holiday. Alice still believed in her marriage and she also believed that Robin's family were fundamentally good people. The problem had been their early years, when Robin was too weak with them. For some reason, he was afraid of them. Afraid of what? she thought, how can being a good parent and setting examples of good behaviour be so difficult? She always took into account the loss of their mum and the re-marriage of their father. Was this the only reason they all behaved so irresponsibly and underhandedly, or did it go much deeper than that?

Should she have become involved with the discipline much sooner? Should she have set boundaries and enforced consequences to their actions? She also knew that she herself was not without faults and was not always the perfect mother or wife. Or come to that, the perfect daughter or friend. No one is perfect, however there is an acceptable level of behaviour and she felt that the line had been crossed many times. It had occurred to Alice that it might be attention seeking behaviour at times, especially from Julie who may be craving the love and affection of her father, and instead was witnessing him giving that attention to his wife. The truth was that Alice had no idea how his relationship had been with the children, and what the family dynamics were like when their mum was alive.

Robin very rarely spoke of how his life was with his first wife, she was not privy to such delicate information. It was such a complicated situation and Alice knew that her recent actions may result in a gentle implosion within the extended family.

Fortunately, she was granted two days' leave that was badly needed. Although she had not viewed the property, Alice had blindly agreed to rent from her friend. Her gut instinct told her the house would be clean and well decorated. She was not disappointed.

The three bedrooms were of a good size and the bathroom was very spacious. There was a deep luxurious bath, a separate power shower and a matching bidet and toilet, the colour scheme was a tranquil shade of pale aqua green which was well balanced with the white bathroom suite.

When she saw the bathroom she was delighted and imagined candlelit soaks.

Checking out the rest of the house, Alice made a mental note of how she could make this a sanctuary for her daughter. The plans were spinning around inside her head, helping to block out the torment of leaving Robin. She convinced herself she was doing the only thing she could.

Time would tell if she had made the right decision.

Although she recognized it was a risky decision, she felt that she was being true to herself and at the same time, proving to her daughter that she would do almost anything to alleviate the intolerable situation her unfortunate daughter was in.

Anne Marie was equally impressed with the house they were about to share, however her own home was her main priority and she knew that by leaving the house, even though it was secure, was still risky while the culprits were at large.

This concern was reinforced the following day when they returned to the property with a van.

The moment Alice parked the Lincoln van on the road adjacent to the lane she had a sinking feeling in her gut. She had the feeling that her daughter was facing even more distress. It was heart breaking as they walked up the garden path with the burnt out gate and scorched garden. The cottage, all boarded up, was a sad sight to see. They followed the path around the side of the cottage, to the back door which Anne Marie had the key for the padlock in her hand, but she needn't have bothered. The plate metal on the back door had been prized off and the back door forced open. The look of horror on her daughter's face tore Alice in two. She called to Ann Marie not to go inside alone, but she was already squeezing through the broken door. Alice gasped as they entered the kitchen. The sink tap was running. Water was overflowing and the kitchen flooded.

The plug had deliberately been left in... All of the electrical appliances had been stolen from the kitchen and the cooker had been ripped out, but was obviously too heavy for them to carry away. They made their way to the lounge and just as expected, everything of value had been taken, including the television.

They were both afraid when they climbed the stairs. In fear of what they would find, but also afraid someone may be up there squatting. As it turned out, very little had changed upstairs, thankfully they were not interested in bedroom fittings.

Together they disassembled the pine bedstead, and all of the bedroom furniture. After loading the bedroom furniture in the van, they carried the two sofas, and the coffee and lamp tables. With the Welsh dresser, they separated the top and bottom and loaded them into the van, not afraid of hard work, they continued until all of Anne Marie's belongings were packed into the van. They were exhausted beyond belief when Alice parked the van outside the place that was to be their temporary new home. Alice's brother Darren had agreed to meet them after he had finished work and true to his word he was waiting for them outside of the house. He unloaded the van with help from his sister, while Anne Marie carried the boxes up the stairs for temporary storage. Darren then fixed the two beds together and assembled the welsh dresser.

Both women were so grateful for his help and were even more grateful when he offered to help Alice transport her own furniture and possessions the following day. He kissed his sister and niece goodnight and told them to get off to bed as they both looked worn out.

And indeed they were. After putting linen on the beds, they had a light supper, then straight to bed. Anne Marie was to be up early in the morning to catch a train into the city for work. Alice had many plans for the day. She would have the house looking like a home and a very special meal ready for her daughter when she arrived back.

The following day, brother and sister removed the furniture that Alice had taken with her to her marital home. Alice was sad, the house looked bare without the large refectory table and chairs.

This was made even worse when the rest of her furniture was removed. All that was left in the lounge was two sofas and a coffee table. She took her ornaments, lamps and her dinner service.

Her entire wardrobe of clothes and shoes, she packed in four suitcases and two holdalls. Alice carefully packed all of her linen, crystal, crockery and kitchen utensils.

Indeed, Alice took away every item she had taken with her to the marital home. She felt so terrible and cruel, removing home comforts from Robin and his family. Every item they had purchased together as man and wife, she left out of loyalty to her husband.

But now it was time to look after herself and her daughter.

The only saving grace for Alice was that Robin's father was not there to witness the event. He was attending a hospital appointment, accompanied by Robin. In addition, none of Robin's family were at home, therefore preventing any embarrassment from both parties.

The whole situation was surreal. Her beautiful home was silent, empty and bare of home comforts. Any evidence that Alice had ever lived there was gone, all packed tightly into a van ready for a new location.

She considered what Robin's father would say when he returned from the hospital, but thankfully fate prevented him from ever knowing that his daughter in law had left his beloved son. For that, Alice was eternally grateful. The consultant decided to admit him to the hospital for further investigations. Sadly within two weeks, and following a number of investigations, he was transferred to a hospice, where he died peacefully six weeks later. In some ways Alice felt relieved that he had never known the awful truth that his son was not only grieving for his father but also for the breakdown of his relationship with Alice.

During the eight weeks he was in hospital, she visited with Robin as a couple and Robin had made it quite clear to his family that they were not to let their granddad know about the situation...

It must have been very difficult to keep this information to themselves, but apparently they managed to.

The very formal funeral was held at the town's crematorium and was attended by many friends and family. Alice stood firmly by Robin's side throughout the funeral and afterwards at the wake. Although she suspected the majority of people attending the service knew about her estrangement from Robin, not one person raised the uncomfortable subject. They were regularly seen together in the village doing the shopping and even going out together occasionally in the evening. In some respects it was like creating a smoke screen for the public at large. Neither of them wanted to air their dirty washing in the public arena. It was to remain private between themselves. Although family and friends were confused with the situation, no one addressed it.

It was an extremely sad day for Robin and his brothers, for they had now lost both of their parents. Alice felt Robin's pain and guessed there would be many emotions going through his tormented mind, not least the memory of his first wife.

She sincerely hoped the memory of that pain was not being reinforced.

She felt responsible for some of the hurt he was going through and needed to remind herself that she too had been hurt and let down.

Saying goodbye to her husband and his family after the funeral and going back to an empty house, was not very comforting for her. She had been granted compassionate leave for the funeral but Anne Marie was not considered close enough family for the same privilege. So Alice was alone with her thoughts. She changed out of her funeral attire and dressed in her most comfortable jeans and a soft warm sweater. Alice made herself a coffee and settled on the sofa.

Sunshine was flooding through the lounge window, giving the room a cheerful feel. She looked around the room. They had made it very cosy with a mix of hers and Anne Marie's belongings.

Surprisingly, she had begun to feel settled in her new home and really made an effort to create a cosy welcoming home. Her brother helped by putting up pretty Roman blinds in the bedrooms and bathroom... He loaned them a few garden tools so they were able to keep the small back garden tidy. Tending the garden was therapeutic for both Alice and Anne Marie. The fresh air and the smell of the earth gave them a connection with life, a natural human instinctive calmness not comparable with other pursuits. The garden was already neat and tidy when they rented the house.

However it lacked colour, so they planted border plants and placed pots of herbs on the patio area. Alice also retrieved a number of her favourite pot plants from her own garden. Robin had been very agreeable to this as he knew how important it was for his wife to have green space around her; he knew how much she enjoyed the garden.

At the far end of the lawn was a small summerhouse with two old fashioned striped deckchairs, in which Anne Marie hung pretty bunting around the windows, giving a seaside feel. It was here Alice enjoyed reading at the weekends when Anne Marie went to visit Andrew.

Some days she took a flask of tea and a packed lunch to the summerhouse and spent hours relaxing, she easily got involved with the characters in the book, soaking up the words and allowing her imagination to run riot. Alice chose fiction that she could identify with, choosing family drama, and romance. Occasionally she read historical novels and was particularly inspired when reading of strong powerful women, who against all odds succeeded against the establishment. Alice felt empowered reading of such women, she herself aspired to be like them, weak women she had no time for, and yet at times Alice considered herself as being weak and she felt ashamed of herself. Her determination to help her daughter was paying off and for this she was grateful. Watching over her daughter reinforced the maternal instincts that was intrinsically part of her personality, however unlike her husband she also knew that her daughter was an adult, not a child and Anne Marie was also an independent young woman who had proved as much by completely supporting herself from a young age. Alice was proud of how Anne Marie was handling the current situation. Although the police had kept in contact with respect to the ongoing investigation into the criminal damage against her, they were unable to assist in other matters. She was still paying the mortgage, utilities and council tax on the cottage. In addition, because she needed to commute much further to work every day, her transport costs had increased dramatically. Selling the house in its current condition would be impossible and the insurance company were dragging their feet. In addition, they were requesting an excess fee for each individual incident which amounted to a considerable sum. Anne Marie had no intention of ever returning to the property to live there, the memories were too painful and she would never feel safe. One option she considered was to rent the property out once the repairs had been completed, however this also was proving difficult. Estate agents and solicitors would need paying and health and safety issues needed addressing. Anne Marie would need a safety certificate and full boiler service for the central heating. The list was endless. After a lot of thought she contacted the bank to review her mortgage situation. Sadly her home had devalued.

This came as no surprise but left her with very little choice. She considered declaring herself bankrupt but was concerned about the implications for her future in terms of getting another mortgage. Already involved in local politics and being aware of the desperate need for more social housing, Anne Marie contacted the local housing department and offered the property at a very realistic price. Thankfully her offer was accepted and after all expenses were paid, she was only in debt by £2000. A manageable amount worth paying to have the peace of mind getting rid of the house, allowing her and Andrew a new start.

Alice was still sat on the sofa in deep thought when Anne Marie arrived home. They had fallen into a comfortable pattern of life together. On work days Alice was always home first, she prepared the evening meal while Anne Marie showered and changed. They shared a bottle of wine every evening while relaxing and chatting about the day's events. Each Friday, Anne Marie, instead of coming back to her mum caught a further train which took her south to Andrew until Sunday evening when she returned, ready for work the next day. Some weekends Alice cooked Sunday dinner for her mum and occasionally invited her friends around. Her brother and sisters also called in for a coffee and chat, but most of the time Alice was alone at the weekends.

Having got into the habit of sharing a bottle of wine during the week with her daughter, Alice continued the same pattern of behaviour Friday and Saturday evenings, although she managed the whole bottle. Sitting alone in a peaceful house was once something she dreamed about, even craved, so why was she feeling so unhappy? The only time Alice felt anywhere close to normal these days was when she was with Anne Marie. Work no longer gave her the same pleasure, even the nights out with her friends didn't help. She regularly turned down the invitations to meet up. Her friends were getting concerned and knowing she was usually at home on Friday evenings they had taken to just dropping in on her, usually bearing gifts of wine, flowers and chocolate. They had called around this Friday with the suggestion of a weekend away to the East Coast and they did not take no for an answer. Alice felt that she could not say no to her friends who were trying desperately hard to help her.

When her daughter enquired if she had enjoyed her weekend, Alice tried to sound enthusiastic about the plans for a weekend away at the coast which they had all agreed was to be the weekend after next. She passed her daughter the mail. Anne Marie eagerly opened an official-looking envelope and whooped with joy as she read the contents.

"Mum, this is such good news, I can hardly believe it, the solicitor has finalised the agreements and the money is to be transferred at the end of business in four weeks' time!" The joy on her daughter's face was a sight to behold. Normally Alice would feel overjoyed at such good news, yet she felt dead inside, and lacked any kind of emotion, she had no choice but to feign happiness. In truth, she lied to her daughter.

The weekend away was entirely organised by her friends to the last detail. Helen did the driving, Kay had booked two twin bed rooms and Carol pre booked a table at a nice restaurant close to the harbour. The journey to Whitby was very pleasant, especially as they drove through the North Yorkshire moors, passing RAF Fylingdale, Grossmont and Goathland. They arrived at the bed and breakfast around midday, and even before any weekend bags were unpacked, the girls ushered Alice to the bar where Helen ordered a bottle of red wine and four glasses. Three hours and four bottles of wine later, they checked into the rooms. Alice was sharing with Kay, but in all fairness it didn't really matter who she shared with, Alice was feeling more detached from reality by the day. After a shower the girls dressed in their most fabulous outfits and hit the town. Alice tagged along, attempting to appear as if she was having fun, she was getting better at acting by the day.

Thinking their friend was having a good time encouraged them to extend the evening's entertainment so Helen suggested they go to a late lounge. Passively Alice went along with the majority. In truth she would prefer to go back to the room and go to bed. At least when asleep her mind eventually closed down. The constant and mindless thoughts that turned around in her head were wearing her down and burning her out. She was getting no emotional peace; her thoughts were all over the place. They were irrational at times which frightened her. Jumbled, mindless images flashed through her mind like an old sepia movie on a constant loop, all the time her mind was in turmoil, she felt as though she was two people: the Alice everyone knew and the other, tormented Alice, who was sinking fast.

Her friends were having such a good time and in their alcohol fuelled condition failed to notice their friend was not looking happy. Eventually and not soon enough for Alice, they returned to the bed and breakfast hotel and wished each other good night. Good night, thought Alice, if only I could have one good night's sleep, then perhaps I could face the day with a more positive mind.

The following morning while the others were sound asleep, Alice took herself off for a walk. Very few people were around as she walked up towards the abbey, it was a sunny but cool morning and as she reached the top of the cliffs the sea breeze made her shiver. The sky was an amazing azure blue, the clouds were scattered and looked like soft cotton wool, slowly moving in the breeze. She tried to remember the cloud categories. As part of her earth science studies during her Open University studies Alice had enjoyed learning about the geography of the land and was especially interested in oceanography; the idea of the earth being so dynamic in a constant state of change had fascinated her. She walked along the edge of the cliffs and looked out to sea. A fishing vessel in the distance was bobbing up and down and the gulls were circling above the boat, hoping to catch a stray fish, no doubt. When she reached a rocky outcrop, Alice sat down to rest. She no longer had much stamina, her legs felt so weak and she seemed to tire more easily. Looking around at the rock formations, she thought about the earth's tectonic plates and sea floor spreading, she thought about earth quakes and volcanoes. Her mind once again became overloaded with thoughts, ideas and past learning. Then she remembered the clouds and looked up. Cumulus, that's it, thought Alice, the cloud is cumulus. And with that thought still in her head, she climbed down the path and made her way back.

Her friends were already in the breakfast room and were most obviously relieved when she joined them. "For goodness sake, where have you been, we have all been so worried about you?" said Helen. The others nodded in agreement. She told them of her walk along the cliffs. The girls looked at one another and did not say a word. Alice had noticed and felt ashamed that she had worried her friends after they were all trying so hard to make her happy. The smell of the breakfast cooking encouraged them all to make their way to the table. Surprisingly, she ate a good breakfast, the walk along the cliffs had given her a good appetite.

They all relaxed for a while after breakfast, in the nice conservatory at the back of the hotel.

There was a wide selection of daily newspapers and magazines so they made themselves comfortable for a couple of hours before setting off on a walk to the harbour. As the day progressed the little town got quite busy, especially around the swing bridge area where a busker had set up his speakers and was drawing quite a crowd. They crossed the bridge over to the narrow streets, with interesting shops full of gothic treasures and ornaments. They spent a long time looking in the shops and they all purchased gifts and souvenirs to take home. Kay suggested they visit the Captain Cooke museum, so they all trooped dutifully around the museum, by which time it was well after two o'clock and their stomachs were beginning to protest.

Unable to wait any longer for food. Carol purchased a small carton of mussels from a street vendor. Within a matter of seconds after her purchase, a huge seagull swept down from the sky behind her and picked up the whole carton of mussels in its beak and carried it off.

It was so funny, the girls began to scream with laughter and finally, Alice found she was laughing too.

"Well, I never," said Carol. "I think we had better go in a restaurant to eat lunch, as no way am I sharing my fish and chips with the gulls." The girls all laughed and agreed it was a very good plan.

For the rest of the day everyone was in good spirits including Alice who had finally been distracted from her own depressing thoughts. On the drive back there was lots of laughter and joviality.

Her friends were happy they had managed to put a smile on Alice's face. In fact, they had a lot to thank that seagull for.

Within three months of renting the house together, Anne Marie had signed all the contracts relating to her house sale and had been offered a job in Sussex. Andrew found a lovely two-bedroom cottage to rent, close to the sea front and it had a little garden to the rear and a small patio.

The weekend Anne Marie came back after viewing the accommodation, Alice took her daughter out to celebrate. First they went to the theatre to watch a production of *Blood Brothers*, following this they enjoyed a meal in a good restaurant together.

At last, the agony of the past few months was over for her daughter. Alice was so happy for her.

Yet her emotions were mixed. Alice was going to miss her so very much. The thought of being alone in the house, estranged from Robin was creating a strange empty feeling inside her, a sensation she was not familiar with. Her mind felt numb, confused and very strange, almost the reverse of euphoric.

On the day Anne Marie moved out. Andrew hired a van and once again her furniture and belongings were moved into another home. A new start, and so well deserved, thought Alice.

CHAPTER SEVEN

After the final farewells, hugs and well wishes, Alice shut the front door. The silence was overwhelming. Standing with her back to the door she surveyed the room, every last part of it, from the ceiling to the floor. Her eyes moved slowly, focusing on the inanimate objects within, solid, unloving, unfeeling objects. The only life in the room came from the clock as the mechanical movements made the familiar ticking sound: tick tock, tick tock. Everything was the same, yet everything was different.

She made her way into the kitchen, yes, that too, was still the same. The same kitchen smells that the bowl of fresh fruit provided to the ambience of the room. But the silence was overwhelming. Alice turned the radio on, it was set to a moderate volume, and she turned it high so as to fill the room with the voices of the radio. A newsreader was telling of more sadness in the world, troubles in other lands, and finally how bad the weather was forecast for the next few days. All doom and gloom.

The tone changed to the music of the seventies which for a brief moment lifted her mood, encouraging Alice to remember the good times in her younger days. With this in mind, she went to her bedroom to search out her old family photo albums, so she could reminisce about past times. Although it was only five o'clock she opened a bottle of wine and even before she closed the page of the last family album, the bottle was empty.

The miserable feelings were drowned out by the alcohol, she felt relaxed and very sleepy, her eyes getting increasingly heavy until she could no longer keep them open.

Alice had just started dozing off when the telephone rang. It was Mathew, enquiring if Anne Marie and Andrew had got off all right. Half asleep and slurring her words, she tried to disguise the drunken stupor she was in.

Mathew was no idiot, but did not want to embarrass his mum by mentioning her very obvious drunken state. Instead he enquired how she was. He reminded her she was a wonderful and supportive mum, who was loved very much. He wished her a very good night and said he would ring again later in the week. Alice was pleased that it had been a brief conversation, she tried to make excuses by saying she was very tired and asked her son to forgive her.

She decided to have a nice soak in the bath as this would surely help her to have a restful sleep.

She took another bottle of wine upstairs and proceeded to fill the bath. Alice poured a large amount of lavender oil in the bath, lit two Yankee fragrant candles and set out a soft white towel. She staggered slightly while getting undressed, wobbling as she took off her underwear.

It crossed her mind that maybe it wasn't such a good idea to have a bath, but common sense had long gone. She poured a large glass of wine and climbed into the bath. The warm water felt like a huge comfort blanket enveloping her entire body, the smell of lavender reminded her of warm summer evenings. Under the influence of alcohol, the world appeared a much nicer place, calm and tranquil with no concerns or worries. Somehow the bad, sad and hurtful worries were unable to come to the forefront of her mind. Her mind almost felt anaesthetised against such thoughts. She rested her head against the back of the bath and closed her weary eyes. That was the last thing that Alice remembered as she drifted off into a deep, alcohol infused sleep.

Fortunately for Alice, the bath plug had not been placed in tight enough, so as she lay in a drunken stupor in the bath, the water slowly dripped out until eventually the bath was completely empty. She woke up cold and shivering. It was four in the morning.

Alice grabbed a towel and climbed into the lonely cold bed, the wet towel still wrapped around her. The following day was Sunday. No alarm for Alice. No one to get out of bed for and certainly no one to please or impress. She thought, why should I bother getting out of bed? What was the point?

She had told Robin not to call round as she expected to be busy all weekend helping Anne Marie but Alice hadn't taken into account how bereft she would feel after her daughter went.

The truth was she had been on an adrenaline high for weeks or maybe months, fuelled by the troubles at home and the very sad events surrounding Anne Marie. So Alice stayed in bed until two o'clock in the afternoon, unbelievably out of character for a woman who was, in the past, up at first light and industrious throughout the entire day and evening for that matter.

What had happened to Alice? The realisation made Alice feel ashamed of herself and she realised this could not continue. But change needed strength and courage, something that seemed to have disappeared long ago with the old Alice.

Catching a glimpse of herself in the mirror, she was shocked at her appearance. Her skin was red and blotchy, her hair was flat, lank and lifeless and she had a look of deep sadness such as that of someone bereaved.

Alice actually did feel bereaved, she had lost her life with Robin and both of her children lived far away, too far for comfort.

Two cups of coffee later, she was feeling alert enough to apply make up to cover her face like a mask. She tied her hair up in a high pony tail, pulling at her temples and forehead, straightening out her sagging face. A dash of perfume and she was good to go. Alice decided to visit her mum. In the past, even the recent past, Alice cooked a Sunday roast, inviting her mum, but recently she had lost the heart to cook. Somehow it wasn't the same anymore.

She walked the short distance to her mum's house, it was only twenty minutes away and she felt sure that the fresh air would do her good, maybe even clear her head and lift her mood.

It was a nice afternoon, the sky was clear and considering it was autumn, the temperature was comfortable.

As she walked along the familiar paths, kicking the brown and gold autumn leaves, Alice thought about the many times she had walked along this familiar path with her father. Every Sunday her father took his daughters for a walk while mum prepared the dinner. He proudly walked, holding his daughters' hands, one each side of him. They were usually dressed the same and always had expensive coats and good quality shoes for their Sunday best.

Alice knew every inch of the familiar route, every crack on the pavement, she recognized every house and garden. Most of the houses had low red brick walls in front. Alice and her sister walked along the walls, feeling brave and bold as they jumped over the gaps where the gates swung between the posts.

How she missed him, her father, he was always a great support to his family and Alice so desperately needed him now. She considered Robin's feelings and guessed that he must still miss his first wife. She realised that with death, love never dies. It lives on and on for eternity.

The opposite is true of divorce. The injured party suffers the loss of love, respect and trust, everything gone forever. Alice was feeling more melancholy than ever.

As she entered her mum's kitchen, the aroma of roast lamb sent her taste buds into action and she suddenly felt hungry.

"Hello, Alice," said her mum, "this is a very pleasant surprise, and would you like to stay for dinner. You know I still cook enough dinner to feed the whole family, and just as well today."

She looked at her mum's smiling face and was unable to speak. Her shoulders shrugged up and down as she shook her head and tears fell down her face. Mascara ran down her cheeks and irritated her eyes, made much worse by the action of rubbing. Her mum enfolded Alice in her warm, loving arms. She felt like a vulnerable little girl lost amongst the stress and anguish that had built over the last few years. Sobbing, Alice explained how sad she felt since Anne Marie had left and how the estrangement from Robin was eating away at her, causing physical pain.

She did not disclose how ashamed she felt in terms of her increased alcohol consumption, after all, it was a temporary situation that would soon be normalised.

Gradually, she calmed down and was able to have a sensible conversation with her mum. Alice said that as yet she had no plans with respect to going back to her home she shared with Robin.

A lot depended on his family with respect to their behaviour and their own plans to move out. Even as she spoke, Alice had no confidence in Robin, after all he had not really supported her to the point that she had felt compelled to move out.

Alice was aware that the repairs from the flood damage were now completed, so to some extent the house was suitable to put on the market. However, she had never discussed this with her husband and in truth she considered it the last option. She loved everything about the home they had so excitedly chose together. Alice had imagined they would all live happily together, working as a team, co-operating with the household costs and management. How naive she had been.

Surprisingly, Alice had not lost her appetite and she even managed the delicious dessert.

There was no hurry to leave with just an empty house to return to, so after helping her mum clear away the dinner pots and pans, they both settled on the sofa to watch a good film. The evening flew by, Alice did not want to leave, so her mum collected fresh bed linen and made up the spare bed in Alice and Dianne's old room. It was a strange night for her has she lay in bed looking up at the familiar ceiling.

The paper mobile she had made at seven years of age was still hanging from the corner beam, swaying gently and slowly rotating round. The floral curtains, hung with perfect pleats were left open. Alice looked out at the clear night sky. The moon was full, catching the light on the thousands of twinkling stars. When she was a child. Alice would get sad and frightened looking up at the night sky. The scripture lessons she had at Sunday school, with all the talk of heaven and pearly gates confused her, because all of the talk about death and leaving loved ones behind was too scary to contemplate, she tried to look high in the sky to see heaven and knew for certain she did not want to die in order to get there.

Her dreams that night were tormenting her, testing her conscience. She formulated a plan.

The following day, she handed in her notice at work with no intention of working the three months' required notice. Her work colleagues were in shock and tried to persuade her to change her mind. It was obvious she was not well and they even suspected that Alice might be heading for a nervous breakdown. The practice manager asked Dr Cosgrove to have a confidential consultation with her, but sadly Alice refused the kind offer, which only further reinforced the surgery staffs' concerns. However, with three more months' notice ahead, they felt compelled to back off for the time being. With plans to keep a close and watchful eye on her.

Alice had always been a popular member of the team.

She was usually light hearted and fun to be with and always a good reliable team member.

Now her face was pale and devoid of expression, almost mask like in appearance. Her pretty hair was in terrible condition and she had lost a lot of weight, her uniform was hanging on her already petite frame. When Alice spoke about her plans to leave, she was almost manic with her conversation and behaviour, much to the distress of her colleagues.

How Alice completed that last shift at work without making any mistakes remained a mystery. It did however, put a great strain on her already depleted mental and physical state.

On arrival home, the first thing she did was to pour herself a very large brandy. Her body was worn out and her mind burned out. The brandy did nothing to ease her anguish, so she poured herself another. She was still wearing her coat and shoes; she hadn't even bothered to remove them.

Alice looked around at the rented house and everything looked distant to her. The pieces of furniture that she had since her first marriage, were just pieces of wood and scraps of fabric, held together by nail and thread. Nothing mattered. Nothing belonged.

She needed to escape. To run away where no one could find her. To sleep a restful sleep. To live a peaceful life. To be calm, happy, loved and cosseted. She didn't like this grown up life with its ups and downs and trials and tribulations. She needed help.

Help came not in human form, but in the shape of a brandy bottle. It took four further brandies to sedate her into the submission of sleep. It was not a restful sleep. Her dreams were intense and full of emotion resulting in her body trembling and twitching. She called out for Robin, but he did not come. He was far away sleeping soundly in their comfortable marital bed, while she tossed and turned on the sofa, with only her coat to keep her warm.

A full bladder called Alice awake and she stumbled towards the bathroom. Her mouth was dry, her tongue sticking to the roof of her mouth. Before she even reached the bathroom, Alice felt her stomach cramp tightly causing her to retch and vomit on the floor.

The force of the vomiting, pressed against her full bladder, releasing its contents. She slumped to the floor, sat amongst the sour vomit and steaming urine. It took her a very long time to muster enough energy to drag herself along the floor until she reached a chair to pull herself up.

Alice sat on the chair, her head hanging down. She felt so ashamed. Her coat and shoes were soaked in urine and vomit. All her clothes beneath were sticking to her. She slowly walked into the bathroom and filled the bath with water. Alice climbed in with all of her clothes on and sat in the water staring into oblivion. She undressed and left the pile of clothes in the water, bobbing up and down around her naked body. Eventually as the water turned tepid and she started to shiver, Alice pulled out the plug. She lay on top of the wet clothes, reached out to the side of the bath for a bath towel, covered herself over and lay in the bath all night. The following morning as the early morning sun shone through the bathroom window, Alice stirred. She remembered nothing of the previous evening's event, but she had a good guess as to how and why she had woken up naked in the bath covered with a towel and surrounded by wet soggy clothes. She climbed out and wrapped a bathrobe around her. Alice rinsed all the clothes, tipped the water out of her shoes then promptly put the whole lot in the bathroom sink, later to be discarded in a black bin bag. She refilled the bath with warm water and gave herself a good wash, removing all traces of urine and dried vomit. Then Alice took herself off to bed, where she stayed until hunger pangs woke her up around midday.

For the remainder of the day she sat around drinking coffee and nursing a very bad hangover.

Around eight o'clock the phone rang. Alice did not feel like talking, she let it go over to answer phone. It was Robin enquiring if Anne Marie had settled in her new home, he said he was treating his family to a two-week holiday in Ibiza, as they had always wanted to travel there.

He was going with them and planned to be in touch on his return. She was so glad not to have answered the phone, goodness knows how she would have responded, the words in her head were bad enough, but to say them out loud would have been sacrilege.

Her mind began to slip out of gear from fifth to neutral, she suddenly felt numb. It was as though her brain had somehow closed down. Then suddenly her mind switched back on into overdrive and while in this strange state of mind, she planned her disappearance.

CHAPTER EIGHT

It was a cold damp morning when Alice put into action the plan for her escape. All night she had been scheming and planning, almost to the point of forming a conspiracy. Robin always said that his wife read too many books and he was possibly right. Even Robin would not understand how distorted his wife's mind had become.

Even to Alice it appeared alien that her mind was taking on such thought processes. At times she felt that someone else had invaded her body and taken away the original woman and replaced her with a sad copy of her former self. She felt gripped in an altered existence. An existence she felt sure would be the ruin of her, but she was being dragged along as though she had no control.

Her self-esteem was low, reinforced by her appearance that was getting worse by the day. She was glad that Robin had not seen her for the past few weeks, it was preferable that way. Let him think of her the way she was. He would never know once she had disappeared.

There was still just under three months left of the rental agreement. Alice wrote out a check for the remainder of the rent, wrote a short note explaining that she was going away on retreat and would be in touch. She requested for Helen to let the rest of the girls know.

The remainder of the letters were far more difficult to write. Despite her confused state of mind, she tried to write with great compassion and love, when writing to her mum and children.

To Robin she simply wrote three words. I LOVE YOU.

The emotion from writing the letters was difficult to cope with. Although it was early, she poured a small amount of brandy into her coffee and settled down to watch the news.

As usual more sadness. The world was full of it, or so it seemed to her. She began to question herself about human nature with all of its frailties and cruelties. The newsreader was announcing that the Catholic church had been aware of the misdemeanours of the priests involved with child sex abuse. The story switched to the cruelty of the nuns in Ireland, particularly to the young unmarried mums. The world was beginning to feel like a very harsh place to Alice. She made another coffee and poured in another measure of brandy.

The plans formulated in her mind overnight now needed to be put into action. She emptied the fridge of its contents, everything except the milk was put in a heavy duty rubbish bag. After cleaning the fridge, she emptied the cupboards of all perishable foods. Everything she put in the dustbin. She filled two large laundry baskets with the remainder of the kitchen contents and left them on the kitchen counter.

After having a shower, she folded the bath and hand towels and all of the bathroom toiletries and placed them inside the laundry basket, keeping behind one towel and a few toiletries which she packed in a holdall. Alice packed two bags in total. One with her clothes and accessories and the other with shoes, toiletries and two bottles of brandy.

With the remainder of the milk she made instant porridge which was to sustain her for the rest of the day. On the refectory table, Alice left out all of the paperwork around the utility bills and house insurance details. Her passport, bank and credit cards she took with her.

After cleaning the house and closing all of the curtains, she took one last look while walking through the front door for the last time, withdrawing from the life which had changed her from a happy, confident outgoing woman, into a depressed shadow of her former self.

Already under the influence of alcohol, she drove to Helen's house and put the letter and spare house keys through the mail box. Then with a heavy heart she drove to her true home, the home that promised so much happiness, the home she shared with Robin. He wasn't in of course. They had all gone off to Ibiza on holiday.

With trepidation, she entered the house. The first thing that struck her was the smell of fresh paint. The building repairs were done and the hallway stairs and lounge had been redecorated as part of the insurance claim.

Alice wandered around the familiar rooms, all still very bare from the lack of furniture and the absence of a woman's touch in terms of cleanliness.

Feeling emotional she went up the stairs, glancing at the sepia photographs on the walls. She went into her bedroom. The beautiful brass bedstead looked inviting, she was tempted to lay down and smell the pillows for a hint of Robin's aftershave. She picked up the crumpled pillow on Robin's side of the bed and hugged it tightly. His familiar scent brought tears to her eyes and she ran out of the room.

She left the letter, the house keys and a spare set of car keys on the kitchen table for Robin. She scribbled a quick note to inform Robin that her car would be parked in the side street behind the railway station. He was to bring it home.

Her mum's house was on route to the railway station but she could not bring herself to call.

Instead, Alice posted the letters to her mum and children. The most difficult and heart searching act she had done that day.

At the railway station, the wind was blowing fierce through the old engine shed that served as a shelter for passengers. She pulled her thick long black coat around herself tightly and pushed her hands deep into her pockets. Alice regretted not having a warm scarf to wrap around her. In the holdall were some decorative scarves but she couldn't be bothered to rummage in the bag.

No one else was around, just as she preferred it to be, she was pleased to be alone, no one around to witness her disappearance from the village she was born into. Surprisingly, even though the surrounding area had developed, it was still a close knit community, and gossip travelled faster than the speed of light. Short of being spotted on the CCTV camera at the station, there would be no other sightings of her, and besides, Alice would be of no interest to someone routinely looking at the footage. She planned to slip into a crowd and disappear.

At this point her destination was uncertain, it was enough for her to know that this was the way out. The train was later than the timetable had indicated, but time was meaningless now. What did it matter?

As she boarded the train, Alice quietly whispered goodbye to the life she was leaving behind.

The journey was uneventful, she stared out of the carriage window the entire journey, lost in total misery and pain, and yet there was a feeling of escape, she knew she was running away instead of facing the truth but felt powerless against her actions.

When the train pulled in to Nottingham Station she had come to a decision as to where she was heading. Her muddled state of mind led her to one possible destination. A place where predictably, most lost souls gravitated towards, usually to find fame or fortune maybe even both, and some went just to disappear. Alice planned the latter.

She had been many times before and had no difficulty locating the platform. The train to St Pancras, London, was due in twenty minutes according to the overhead display. Just enough time to purchase a one-way ticket. Alice journeyed to London. Why there remained a question, she would ask herself many times.

The train sped south as she sat numbly in her seat, staring at everything and nothing, taking her to an uncertain future. The rattle of the buffet cart broke her gaze from the window. In desperate need of a drink she ordered a coffee, nothing more. Her appetite had disappeared a long time ago. She rummaged in her holdall and took out a bottle of brandy, fortunately she had been given a short measure of coffee, enabling her to pour a large measure into the polystyrene beaker. The train manager announced the imminent arrival into London St Pancras, at which point she still had no plans as to where she was going or what she was planning to do in London.

Alice stepped onto the platform. It was three pm. The station was buzzing with commuters, all with a destination in mind, thought Alice, each of them more aware of their future than she would ever be.

Alice began to feel weak and shaky; her legs didn't feel strong enough to support her. She headed for a bench to sit on. The sheer effort of carrying her holdalls had drained the little energy she had remaining. An elderly gentleman came and sat beside her. He tried to make conversation but his voice seemed to be coming from a different direction than his lips, she felt most strange, almost spaced out. The gentleman passed her a sweet in its wrapper, she realised that perhaps her blood sugar levels were low and contributing to her confused state. She smiled kindly at the gentleman and unwrapped the sweet, popping it into her mouth. He tipped his hat towards Alice and bid her farewell. How kind, she thought, somehow he knew that she needed glucose to abate the trembling and shaking of her hands. Perhaps he was a diabetic and recognized the symptoms of a hypoglycaemic attack.

The only reason her own levels were low was that she had not eaten for a very long time and the alcohol had brought down her glucose levels. This was also contributing to her confused state of mind. For some strange reason she really didn't care. The body and mind of Alice, which she had so carefully nurtured, was no longer of any importance or consequence to her. She wanted to think of nothing, no one and not even herself. The only way she could achieve this was to head to the nearest bar to drown out the horrible feelings and thoughts churning around inside the body and mind of someone named Alice.

The nearest bar was in fact a hotel, which turned out to be a blessing in disguise, for after purchasing four double brandy and lemonades she desperately needed a bed to rest on.

The hotel had a single room available so she checked in for two nights, which eventually turned into ten nights and Alice could be found every afternoon in the lounge bar until she was drunk enough to fall asleep, which on a number of occasions, occurred in the bar, much to the disdain of the hotel manager.

The next time she tried to extend her stay, she was told the room was no longer available and the hotel was fully booked. She understood why, and didn't make a fuss. Instead she quietly packed her holdall with her now dirty clothes and headed towards the nearest launderette.

This was not easy, as a result she needed to frequently ask for directions and after three long hours of walking around, probably in circles, going by some of the obscure directions given to her, Alice found herself in the Camden Lock area of London. Finally, she located a launderette, where she sat watching her dirty clothes spin round and round. The steady rhythm and sound of the washing machine calmed her down.

She suddenly felt the need to contact her family, but unable to summon the courage to speak to them, Alice sent them a text message. She simply wrote, "Don't worry, be happy. I love you Xxx" she then switched off the mobile phone to conserve the battery.

When the washing was dry, she set to folding her clothes to pack. It was while she was packing the clothes into her holdall that Alice noticed an advertisement pin board. A picture of a canal boat was pinned to the board. Intrigued, she took a closer look. It appeared that the boat was available to rent and was moored close to the Camden Lock area. It was rather pricey, but for the first time in days Alice felt a glimmer of hope; she could see a direction in which to head.

A flutter of excitement rose in her heart. Without hesitation, she switched her mobile back on.

Her phone beeped to show that she had four text messages awaiting to be viewed. Alice had a good idea who they were from and delayed answering, hoping to give them good news when she did so. With this in mind she promptly rang the contact number for the boat. She was holding her breath, not daring to breathe. Thankfully her call was answered swiftly and she found herself talking to a very pleasant sounding lady by the name of Sally.

The boat was indeed still available and Sally arranged to meet Alice later that afternoon. She provided the directions and arranged a time suitable to both of them.

Full of expectation, Alice made her way towards the canal. Walking along the towpath triggered a mixture of emotions: sadness, anticipation, confusion and hurt.

She was well aware of her appearance and how unkempt she looked. She had lost a lot of weight and her clothes were hanging on her loosely. Her hair was in poor condition as a result of her recent unhealthy diet. Alice asked herself, would she rent a boat to someone like herself?

Probably not! With time to spare she called into a café, ordered a coffee and toasted tea cakes and then used the facilities to smarten herself up. She changed into a pair of freshly laundered Capri pants and a tunic top. Although the top was very loose, by wearing a wide leather belt she managed to pull the outfit together. She changed into a pair of ballerina pumps, put a bright scarf around her neck and put on some gold hooped earrings.

Alice swept her hair up into a high ponytail and gripped it in place with an enamel clip. She applied a little make up, a splash of perfume and was good to go.

As Alice was approaching the canal boat she began to feel anxious. Beads of sweat began to form above her upper lip and the salty taste seeped into her mouth.

In the distance she saw a rather flamboyant lady swiftly walking in her direction. By the time Alice had reached the rather delightful boat, the lady had managed to catch up with her. She said, "I guess you are the lady I spoke with earlier?" Alice nodded timidly as she shook the extended hand offered to her, announcing herself as Sally, the owner of the boat.

It turned out, Sally normally lived aboard and had recently been offered the opportunity to work on an assignment in the Netherlands and would be away for at least three months, during which time she had hoped to rent out her home to someone she could trust.

Alice hoped against all odds that Sally would find her trustworthy, which indeed she considered herself to be. The name of the boat was *Poppy*; it was a fifty-five foot semi traditional canal boat with a reverse layout. Therefore, the galley was at the stern. The boat exterior was painted a deep blue with sprays of poppies painted on either side of the boat cabin. The front (bow) of the boat had a canopy over a cratch providing an area with a small bistro table and a chair. A vase of flowers stood cheerily on the table centre and a short clothes line was strewn across the top cross bar of the cratch…

They entered the boat at the stern end down two sturdy steps, immediately leading into a delightful galley area, comprising of a full size calor gas cooker, a full size fridge and a small sink unit. There was a fabulous bespoke dresser, full of blue and white ceramic crockery. It is enchanting, thought Alice and more than ever she wanted to be offered the chance to rent this amazing boat. A peninsular unit with a glass upper cabinet separated the galley from the lounge/diner which had a small sofa bed covered with pretty scatter cushions, a lamp table a small footstool and a gate leg table with two fold up chairs. A wood burning stove surrounded by a slate earth was the focal point of the room and a large brass coal scuttle full of coal and logs was set to the side. A flat screen television stood on a narrow book case that was overflowing with books. The floor throughout the boat was oak laminate boards with pretty wool rugs scattered about. The lounge/diner was separated by an open door leading through to a narrow passage.

On the left was a door leading into the bathroom consisting of a white cassette toilet, vanity basin and small shower. Further along the narrow passage was a cosy bedroom. The three quarter fixed bed looked so welcoming.

Above the bed were fixed cupboards with under lighting, a fitted wardrobe completed the room which led out to two small French doors and the cratch area containing the bistro table set. It was so delightful, so charming.

Sally put the kettle on the stove and beckoned Alice to sit with her awhile on the sofa. "It will take a while for the water to boil," she said. "Perhaps we can take the time to get acquainted with each other." Sally was pleasantly surprised to hear that Alice was well accustomed to the inland waterways, having spent many happy hours cruising the Grand Union, the Trent and Mersey and Leeds Liverpool canals. Without trying to pry too much, Sally enquired as to why Alice needed to rent the boat.

Alice hesitated and considered how much she should disclose about herself and decided that Sally only needed to know the basics. She told Sally a little about herself in terms of the work she loved and the many hobbies she enjoyed. She told her a little about Robin, her own children and four step children. Concluding that basically she was on retreat having recently been through an unusually stressful time and was hoping to spend some time alone to regain her strength and appetite for life. This explanation appeared to satisfy Sally. However, Sally then dropped a bombshell, by requesting a character reference. The anguished look on Alice's face told Sally everything she needed to know. "So let's start again," said Sally in a very reassuring voice. The combination of the nostalgia being on the boat, physical and mental exhaustion and the friendly voice of Sally triggered an overwhelming emotion deep inside her heart and for the first time in months, Alice cried, letting out the deep pain and sadness. A river of tears flowed from her tired eyes, tears and emotion that had been banked up for months waiting to escape.

The adrenaline and cortisol high that had buoyed her along through the months of stress was no longer able to sustain her. She allowed the tears to cleanse the pain.

The kettle whistled, beckoning Sally, who went to make a pot of tea, giving Alice time to collect her emotions.

Sally opened up the gate legged table, setting it with a blue and white tea set. She placed down a matching two tier cake stand filled with a variety of cakes in the centre and matching side plates.

She beckoned Alice to join her at the table. This time Alice told her everything. Well, almost everything. It felt good to be honest and open with Sally, in addition it was a relief to get everything off of her chest, almost liberating. Sally listened carefully and never interrupted or passed comments.

Throughout the conversation Alice realised how much she was missing her friends, and although it had not yet been two weeks, it occurred to her, how helpful it is to have a shoulder to cry on. They drank the tea in silence, Alice had no appetite for cake, but out of respect for Sally she chose the smallest cake and slowly forced it down. This did not go unnoticed; Sally had seen the sadness in Alice within the first few moments of meeting her. She had also observed that the clothes she was wearing, although cleverly disguised, were hanging about her small frame. Her expression gave away the emotional pain, Sally knew that look, for she had seen the same expression in her own reflection. She had been there herself. Sally had her own demons and her own past problems. Not wishing to protract the anxiety any longer, Sally offered her hand to Alice. They shook hands as Sally announced, "You have yourself a home for three months." The relief on Alice's face was a sight to behold. They agreed that Alice would pay two months' rent in advance and if she needed to stay a further month, the balance could be paid on Sally's return.

Sally preferred cash payment which amounted to £2000, an amount not available from a cash machine so off they walked back along the towpath into town to find the nearest National Westminster bank where Alice cashed in her own personal ISA. Originally, this was set aside for Robin and herself to go on a Mediterranean cruise when they retired, but her immediate needs were now much more important. The ISA along with the interest made was enough to pay Sally and to provide enough money for Alice to live off for the next few months. Additionally, by using her own savings instead of taking money from the joint account, she left no audit trail for Robin to know where she was.

They returned to Poppy. Sally packed her belongings into two suitcases. She then demonstrated how to work the cooker, the diesel central heating and the water pump. She showed Alice where the spare calor gas was stored and how to safely change the canister.

Sally pointed out where the nearest water point and sanitation unit were located, adding that it would be the only occasion that Alice needed to move the boat on to the water pump and sanitary unit, then it was to be returned to the fixed mooring spot which had been hooked up with electricity. She demonstrated how to start the engine and how to grease the stern gland close to the engine. Having agreed to the terms and conditions Alice signed the contract and handed the required cash to Sally.

They shook hands on the deal, each having their own copy of the agreement.

Sally bid Alice farewell and good luck adding a request for her beloved *Poppy* be taken great care of. It was getting on for six o'clock when Alice finally got around to looking at her text messages. The first was from Anne Marie saying she understood her mum's need to escape and seek solace, but she felt partly responsible for adding extra stress and anxiety into her mum's already difficult life.

She enquired as to where her mum was staying and begged her to keep in touch. Mathew's text was along the same lines except in addition he added that he would be away in the USA for the next 6 weeks and had asked his sister to keep him informed. Of course, neither of them were aware of the true extent of their mum's deteriorating mental health and her increasing alcohol dependence. The third text was from her mum, it was full of worry and concern. She told her daughter to come home and live with her until things had settled. The fourth was from Robin. It simply said. "Come home." Alice wrote one message and sent to all. She said, "I am fine and have found a tranquil place to stay, surrounded by water. I need to rest and recover before I return.

"There is nothing left of me to give you. I need to build up my reserves. Forgive me. I love you."

She switched off her mobile phone and looked around at her surroundings. Perfect.

Although not hungry, Alice knew she needed to eat. Sally had told her to use up any food stored in the fridge and cupboards. It was too late to go to the shop and she was not familiar with the area and where she might find a late opening shop, so Alice searched the dresser. She found a tin of soup and crackers, which were just about manageable for her to eat. She warmed the soup and made herself comfortable on the sofa. Balancing a tray of soup and crackers on her lap, she found the remote control and switched on the television. The news was on and as usual pictures of starving children in Africa were flashed across the screen along with talk of impending wars and recent disasters. It was all so heavy and depressing. Her brain felt so dead and exhausted these days, as though there was no capacity for it to absorb any new knowledge. Her brain needed a rest and the only way to switch off the constant thoughts turning around in her head was have a drink of alcohol. She rummaged in her holdall and pulled out half a bottle of brandy, pouring herself a large measure. Having drunk the last drop, she rested her head against the sofa and closed her eyes. The sounds of the evening drifted by, she heard young couples walking along the towpath talking of love and hope. She heard teenagers laughing and joking with each other. Alice felt so far removed from these people, removed from reality. She felt like an insignificant piece of dust, a nobody. Someone to be ignored. She poured another large brandy, hoping the negative thoughts about herself would quieten down or even disappear. It took two more measures before her mind was too numb to register any emotion, at which point she staggered to the bathroom, which was pointless, as she could not be bothered to have a wash or clean her teeth.

What did it matter anyway? She had no one to impress, who cared? She certainly didn't. She used the toilet and washed her hands; some things were still important. Alice snuggled down in the comfort of the bed, the gentle rhythmic rocking of the boat lulled her to sleep. She must have been exhausted, for it was past ten thirty when she awoke. The cabin was still dark except for a tiny beam of light escaping into the hatch door. The porthole covers had blackened out the cabin to such an extent one would never know day from night on a dull day.

She removed the porthole covers in the bedroom allowing bright light to flood into the cabin.

Alice made a coffee and settled on the sofa where she sat for a while in her pyjamas, staring out of the window which was just above the level of the towpath. A dog walker went by, calling his dog, then a cyclist, followed by an elderly couple holding hands. Life goes on all around, thought Alice, although she did not feel a part of it. She almost felt as though she was trapped in a bubble, screaming to get out. Eventually she got dressed and tied her hair into a ponytail, Alice was afraid to look in a mirror for fear of what her reflection was like. She could tie her hair back with her eyes shut, it. Anyway did it matter how she looked? No one knew her in this vicinity.

They did not know the vibrant well-groomed Alice, that was. She was of no interest to anyone. She could get lost in the crowds and become almost invisible. With this in mind, she stepped off the boat into strange yet familiar territory, for in some respects the inland waterways were her sanctuary. Being surrounded by water usually had a calming effect on her, some would say that her birth sign of Pisces reinforced her love of the water. This would need to be a very potent effect to help her through the next few weeks. Although a little cool, the sun was shining brightly resulting in the muddy water of the Grand Union glistening as the sun's rays caught tiny droplets of water. She noticed there were four other boats on the long stay moorings.

A young woman was hanging washing on a rotary airer attached to the stern of her boat. She greeted Alice good morning and she responded with a cheery wave. Living on a boat in the centre of London was affordable living for young couples struggling to afford a mortgage or the extortionate rents that landlords were charging. Alice had empathy for the young people trying to make a living in such austere times. She reflected on how easy it had been for her generation in the sixties and seventies to secure a job. In the late sixties and early seventies there was still a lot of manufacturing in the Midlands. If one didn't enjoy the work, it was easy enough to move within days to another job. Alice was unable to start her nurse training until the age of eighteen so she had been able to choose an alternate job of her choice without too much trouble.

Alice walked along the now busy towpath. A sign for Camden market caught her attention, so she made her way in that direction. The area was vibrant, buzzing with people, by the look of it, mostly tourists. There was an array of stalls and quaint shops. However, Alice was on the lookout for a certain type of shop. One that sold alcohol. Although she needed to budget sensibly over the next few weeks, she was still prepared to pay for anything to help numb the torment in her once again buzzing head. Besides, she was feeling a little shaky, and the alcohol usually helped to calm these feelings down. Alice spotted a Tesco Direct store. That was good news, she could use her Tesco club card vouchers towards the cost of her shopping. Unfortunately, the discount voucher read that in order to save £5 she needed to spend £40. Logically Alice decided to purchase two bottles of brandy. Why not! And that is exactly what she did. In addition, Alice purchased:

bread, milk, cheese, butter and four tins of soup. Enough to carry, thought Alice. She made her way back to the boat and made herself a coffee to which she added a good measure of brandy. It was not yet midday.

Alice unpacked her belongings. Sally had very kindly made space in the wardrobe and drawers, plenty of room for her clothes. She organised her underwear and assortment of accessories including scarves and jewellery. The few toiletries she had left were placed in the bathroom cabinet. Satisfied with a job well done, she prepared herself some breakfast. Her appetite was still quite poor, so she made one slice of buttered toast. Sat on the sofa, opposite the overflowing book case, she checked out the titles and noted there was a lot of reference books and a few classic novels. She chose a classic by John Fowls, *The French Lieutenant's Woman*. She put her feet up on the sofa and began to read about Sarah Woodruff and her lost virtue. Normally a very avid reader, Alice would absorb every word and statement, she could get lost in a story and believe in the characters. Although the story was developing into an interesting read, it was not enough to distract her thoughts completely, she still needed help to relax. Three double brandies later, Alice was asleep on the sofa; a pattern of behaviour that continued over the next five weeks. Except for a visit to the shop, Alice became a recluse on the boat, reading, drinking, sleeping, and occasionally warming a tin of soup.

CHAPTER NINE

Alice had been missing for over a month. Her friends had been in contact with Robin and her mum for news. Her mum had turned to Alice's brother and sisters for moral support. Mathew and Anne Marie were frantic with worry. Alice was no longer answering her phone.

The reality was that she was sinking fast, just as a vessel can sink when overburdened with water, she was sinking from her depth of depression and anxiety. She was spiralling into a claustrophobic and suffocating depth of despair, with no life belt to cling on to. Alice had developed a vast collection of related mental illnesses: anxieties, phobias and compulsive behaviour. She was rendered powerless by her alcohol dependence, a dependence that required a regular supply of brandy which she was finding difficult to afford. Each day she counted her money, not like a miser, more like a street beggar. On the days Alice left the security of the boat to go to the market, she spent very little on food, only the barest amounts, just enough to sustain her weakening body. She was hanging on to her declining savings by purchasing the cheapest and highest alcohol content drinks to help control the withdrawal symptoms she had recently begun to experience when her blood alcohol levels declined.

It was on one such visit that Alice decided to venture a little further along the canal cut. Feeling a little less apprehensive, somewhere deep in her reserves, a small spark of enthusiasm was emerging, a tiny flicker of the old Alice. This was enough to keep her walking further and further away from her normal route. Her gait was of a despondent, tired middle aged woman as she slowly put one foot in front of the other. Her loss of muscle mass and the increasing joint pains as a result of the build-up of uric acid in her joints made for a slow and steady plod along the towpath.

Not used to walking the extra distance, Alice noticed she was more short of breath than usual and in addition had developed an irritating cough. She had been suffering from severe acid reflux for weeks, likely associated with the increased acid in her gut from the alcohol. Searching deep into her mind and trying to recall her medical knowledge, she decided that the acid reflux was irritating her throat causing the cough. She continued walking and what for others would have been a glorious scene beside the tranquillity of the water and the pretty decorated boats moored along the towpath, for Alice it was a painful reminder of times past when Robin and she took their own boat along the inland waterways. A time when they were both full of enthusiasm for life and each other. What amazingly good times they had shared. Robin always planned an interesting scenic route, usually ending the day with a mooring close to a canal side inn or pub.

Alice sometimes took control of the tiller, but more often she was responsible for opening and closing the lock gates as they travelled to higher or lower ground. She enjoyed chatting to other boaters at the locks while waiting for the water to rise or fall. Although hard and demanding work it was most enjoyable, the bonus, of course, had been the weight bearing activity and pushing against the lock gates helped to strengthen her core muscles and develop the muscles in her arms and legs. She was reminded of this when approaching "Dead Dog Basin" a well-known post-industrial area, riddled with tunnels for the old boats carrying goods into London. Alice sat on an old bench to catch her breath and rest her weary feet. She began to cough until her sides ached, a further paroxysm resulted in Alice coughing up a large amount of rusty coloured sputum. Scattered on the floor around the bench she noted cigarette butts and empty lager cans. A faint whiff of alcohol drifted towards her nostrils, sending a shiver down her spine and a longing for alcohol. The dependent receptors in her brain were sending messages she could not ignore.

The demons won.

Alice turned around and made her way back to Turnover Bridge and Hampstead Road lock number one. Back to the bohemian markets and more important, to a supply of Scrumpy cider she could purchase by the litre. The day was drawing to a close, she was weary and feeling unwell. A short distance from the boat, Alice sat down under a bridge, her legs drawn up beneath her.

The ground was damp, she didn't care, and her trousers soaked up the moisture, the cold and clingy clothes made her shiver. Above her, perched on the bridge supports, pigeons roosted. The ground beneath thick with pigeon guano, the smell was repulsive and yet she had no desire to move. After all, there was still another bottle of cider to drink.

Eventually she succumbed to sleep. The beautiful, kind, caring Alice was asleep huddled in a corner underneath a bridge. To the rest of the world she looked like a lost soul, a sad vagrant alcoholic. No one would ever have guessed that she had a loving family and friends who were desperately worried about her. They had now reported her missing. The police were now involved.

Anne Marie and Mathew were desperate to find their mum. Their gut feelings were not positive, despite their mum's last message telling them that she was in a tranquil place, close to water. Neither of them were convinced. Everything was wrong. The whole scenario was out of character, what had happened to their wonderful mum? She had always been there for them, supporting them and encouraging, she given everything of herself. The very fact that she had made no effort to contact them, was proof enough. Their mum must be ill, or in an intolerable situation she could not escape from. How close to the truth they were. Alice was in a situation she could not escape from.

Alice woke in the early hours of the morning soaked in sweat and urine. She knew she could not sink any lower. Her state of mind was influenced by alcohol, depression and anxiety.

The root of the problem had been the day she walked out of her beautiful home because her husband had failed her when she had needed his support most.

Meanwhile, Robin had also re-run the many family dramas through his own tormented mind, over and over again. The images playing over in his mind like a re-run of a movie. He constantly questioned himself over and over again. Should he have done things differently? He loved his wife and felt that he had failed her. Since the day he found her car keys through the door, he had thought she was just being her usual strong-willed self. But had he missed something, was it much more? He remembered with pride how she had worked hard to keep the home clean and cooked delicious meals for the family, the sacrifices she made and support to him over the loss of his first wife. They had been soul mates, lovers, husband and wife. Where was she? The doubts began to creep in when she had not responded to his text messages. Robin searched his mind for evidence of previous unusual behaviour she may have displayed in the few weeks before her sudden departure. The truth was, he had taken his family away on holiday. Perhaps this was a big mistake. Likely it was Alice who was most in need of a break. He vaguely remembered that her appetite was declining and she had lost weight. In addition, she was drinking more alcohol. Was this perhaps the key? Everyone had a breaking point, had Alice reached hers the day she left?

Alice forced herself to stand, first of all by kneeling on all fours and then pushing up with her hands, she was weak to the point of collapse and felt very breathless. Her instinct told her that she urgently needed help. Her chest felt so tight, it hurt. Alice slowly walked along the towpath, every step took a great deal of effort, every breath felt like the last. Her respirations were rapid and rasping.

Just ahead of her, Alice saw her temporary home, the brightly painted *Poppy* came into view.

Alice somehow managed to climb over the gunwales and into the bow of the boat. Then she remembered no more.

Robin had not seen Mathew and Anne Marie for many weeks and this was not a good meeting place. Together they sat in front of the young police officer and presented him with a current photograph of Alice. How could a stranger understand their pain? How were they to describe the love they felt for Alice? His questions were searching and at times embarrassing for Anne Marie and Mathew. No, mum was not having an affair or involved in criminal activity and she certainly was not running away from someone. Robin was equally alarmed to be questioned about potential domestic violence and abuse. They were questioned about any family arguments or disputes. No conclusions were drawn. The young police officer tried his best to reassure them that most missing people are eventually found. He requested access to their mobile phones to trace the last messages from Alice and advised that he would contact them if any progress was made. Robin invited Anne Marie and Mathew to join him and his family for a meal. This was not easy for them to accept, Robin understood this. It was very painful for them to return to the home their mum loved. They both headed straight to the conservatory and sat there in silence. This was their mum's favourite room. Anne Marie looked out at the garden. It was now neglected, the love and care their mum had bestowed on her garden was long gone. Weeds were growing high in the borders; the lawn was overgrown. It appeared that Robin had lost interest in the garden since his wife had left. Anne Marie began to cry. Her mum was her rock, she felt adrift and vulnerable.

Mathew held his sister in his arms and tried to comfort her. Meanwhile Robin was busy in the kitchen preparing a meal for his family and step children. They heard voices, as Julie and Gary arrived home. They were in good spirits, laughing and joking with each other.

Robin called out to them, enquiring if they had a good day. It appeared they had both taken the day off work to visit a theme park. Robin informed them that Mathew and Anne Marie were here and it might be nice if they were offered some refreshment. He asked Julie to put the kettle on. Reluctantly she did as her father requested. She was aware of the disappearance of their mum, but hadn't paid much attention. After all, her life had been easier since her step mum left, she was the woman of the house now. The downside being that she was surrounded by four men. The house was not as clean or organised and the meals basic. The boys still argued constantly and her dad continued to run around after all of them. Her father though, for most of the time, was sad and lonely. He worked long hours away from home and slept in late at the weekend. This was the best of it, they often had the house to themselves so they regularly had friend around for heavy drinking sessions. But the excitement of this freedom was wearing thin.

As Julie approached the conservatory, she was alarmed to see her step sister crying and Mathew looking sad and defeated. It was at this precise moment that reality struck her, like the pain she felt when she was told of her own mum's illness. Julie felt sick with remorse. Anne Marie managed a weak smile in response to the offer of a drink. Mathew asked for something a little stronger than tea. Wayne arrived half an hour later followed by a very moody Stephen who had apparently been reprimanded at work for some kind of misconduct. The boys spoke briefly to their step brother and sister, then settled in front of the television until Robin called that dinner was ready. Mathew noticed that his mum's furniture was back in the house with the exception of the glass topped coffee table. Robin told Mathew that the house Alice had been renting, needed clearing for new tenants, so with the help of the boys, he hired a van and returned all of Alice's possessions back home.

"What about Mum's clothes and jewellery?" enquired Anne Marie.

"All of her personal possessions are safe and packed away in boxes," replied Robin.

"And Mum's coffee table?" asked Mathew.

"Ah, well, sadly that was damaged during the move," answered Robin.

No more was said about their mum's precious belongings. Mathew noted that Robin was running around after his family as usual, the sad fact was that his family expected it. On the surface Robin appeared to be getting on with his life but Mathew had noticed his step father did not look well. He knew Robin would be burying his head in the sand instead of facing up to the situation, as he had always done. Likely his family were enjoying living with their father, who they could easily manipulate in any way they chose. But this was his mum's home. Where was she? After the meal, Anne Marie offered to clear away the dishes, but Robin would not hear of it. He enquired if they planned to stay overnight. At this suggestion Mathew noted a lot of feet shuffling and sighs from his step brothers and he was tempted to take up the offer if for no other reason than to stake claim on his own family home. However, he graciously refused on behalf of both of them.

"Actually we appreciate the offer, but we are going visit Gran and spend the night with her," said Mathew. Anne Marie was pleased they had previously arranged this, as she could not bear to spend another second in the house that her mum had worked so hard for, knowing it had been the tremendous pressure put on her shoulders from her step siblings and the lack of support from her husband that was likely the reason her mum had disappeared. They thanked Robin for the meal and said they would keep in touch.

It was only a short journey to their Gran's house, throughout the journey they discussed their views about the reception they had received from their step family. The joint decision they arrived at was of absolute and total lack of empathy from Robin's children with respect to their contribution to the disappearance of their mum. Alice said she had noticed a slight change of temperament in Julie and just maybe like an infection, this change would spread to the boys.

They agreed to keep the situation close to their chests and not to mention their concerns to Gran.

She was already worried sick about her daughter, what good would further worry do? They decided to inform her that the police were hopeful and they said that there was probably a simple explanation as to why their mum had recently lost contact. Although this sounded highly unlikely, they planned to do their utmost to alleviate further worry. Without giving false hope they planned to make their visit a special time with their Gran. Alice's mum was thrilled to see her grandchildren, immediately rushing around to make drinks and providing a selection of her own baked cakes and scones. Gran was at her happiest feeding her family, and although neither Anne Marie nor Mathew were hungry, they accepted the cakes out of politeness. No way would they offend their lovely gran. She told them of her daughter's last visit shortly before leaving.

With sadness in her eyes she told them how their mum had slept overnight in her childhood bedroom and what a thrill it had been for herself, knowing that Alice was back in her childhood home, even though it was for a short while. Their gran did not want to go into detail about how distraught their mum was on this visit, or how tired and depressed she appeared. Instead they spoke of the good times, of when Grandad was alive and how Mathew and Anne Marie spent many happy weeks at the seaside with their grandparents in the school holidays.

After a light supper, they sat together around the kitchen table, looking at old photographs, precious memories of times gone by.

Mathew and Anne Marie had seen the photographs many times before, however this time they were looking from a different perspective, instead of a fleeting glance they looked closely at their mum. They saw her as a little girl, carefree and splashing in a paddling pool at the seaside, a tin bucket in her hand, no doubt collecting water. They looked at every official school photograph, which captured the young Alice over time, growing from a young girl and developing into a teenager. The saddest of all, were the wedding photos of their mum and dad.

She was a young, radiant bride, full of love for their father. The family photographs were hard to bear, as they reminisced over the pictures of themselves as children with both parents. But it did not last. Their mum survived the heartache of a broken marriage. Surely, whatever the problem was now, their mum would overcome it. They knew that fundamentally she was strong and determined. She would get back on track for certain.

Alice could hear mumbled voices that seemed to be coming from afar. Her eyes were so heavy, almost as though they refused to open against her will. Had someone placed lead weights on her lids while asleep? Her chest felt tight and rigid, her breathing shallow. Suddenly she had an overwhelming fear of suffocating and began to panic. In doing so she realized that her left hand was restrained, what was happening? Her mind began to do strange things, swirls of light flashed in front of her eyes, she felt detached from her body, unreal and dream like.

The voice became clearer. "Alice, Alice, are you awake?" Sheer determination aided her to open her heavy eyelids for a few seconds, her vision was bleary as she attempted to focus in the direction of the voice. She did not recognise her location, but knew for sure that she was on a hospital ward. Alice attempted to raise herself up the bed, as two strong arms were placed around her gently and lifted her up the bed.

Almost at once her breathing was a little easier. She cleared her throat and tried to speak. "I am your primary nurse," he said with a smile. Her lips were dry and cracked, her mouth sore.

"What happened?" she said.

"Don't worry about that now, how would you like a nice cup of tea? We need to get some fluids back inside you, get your electrolyte balance stable. Your lips look so parched. I will bring you an oral toilet tray with mouth wash before the tea, otherwise the tea will taste even worse than usual," said Nurse Monroe.

"Thank you," said Alice. "That will be very nice, may I have mint tea please?"

"No problem," he said. "Back in ten minutes." He gave her a small glass of water and placed an oral toilet tray and mouthwash on a bedside table which he positioned in front of her. He gave Alice a wink and told her that mint was not regulation hospital tea but he had an idea where he could source a tea bag.

True to his word, he returned with the mint tea, which apparently he had obtained from a work colleague after a little sweet talk. Alice smiled, she liked this young man. Refreshed and a little more alert, Alice noticed that she was attached to an IV line. The drip stand held two bags, one she recognised as dextrose saline, the other a small bag of saline had a label attached. She guessed it was probably antibiotics. The cannula site at the back of her hand felt uncomfortable, but she knew that once her fluid intake had improved, the IV fluids and antibiotics would be discontinued and oral antibiotics commenced. She felt very weak and still confused as to what had happened for her to be in hospital. She really could not remember anything. Where was Robin? Did he know that she was in hospital? Alice started to cough, a deep, painful cough that came in spasms, she felt her lungs were congested, almost solid as though they had turned to concrete. No matter how hard she coughed she was unable to expectorate any mucus, even though she felt as though she was drowning in fluid. The coughing episode left her exhausted, she lay back on the pillow and began to cry.

"Now then, young lady, we will have none of that." She looked up to see a doctor was at the end of her bed looking through her observation charts. He was very agreeable to the eye. Tall, dark and very dashing, he had a twinkle in his eye when he spoke to Alice. He told her that the charts indicated her temperature was improving, although still raised it was no longer at a serious value. He told her that her respiration rate was now near normal.

"And my oxygen saturation levels, doctor?" enquired Alice.

He cocked his head to one side and with a cheeky grin he said, "Ah, I see that I am speaking with a fellow professional, or a very knowledgeable patient." Alice forced a smile.

"In a former life I was a registered nurse, having worked in both primary and secondary care," she replied. He informed her that her oxygen levels were satisfactory considering that she had pneumonia. That certainly got her attention. He told her that a very nice lady by the name of Sally had found her on the front of a boat. This information jogged her memory. So she had managed to get back to the boat, she must have spent the whole day and the following night exposed to the elements. But surely, Sally wasn't due back yet? Gradually, Alice remembered almost everything and she was ashamed of herself. How could she even begin to tell this handsome doctor how and why she had fallen from grace into the clutches of the demon alcohol? He interrupted her thoughts.

"We have some rather unusual blood results, Alice." She looked embarrassed, for she had a good idea what he was referring to. She was absolutely right.

He said he had expected a raised white cell count and C-reactive protein, but her liver function results were hard to explain. He enquired about her previous medical history, her family history and if she suffered from any sensitivities or allergies. Skirting around the real question, he enquired if she had recently been abroad. Then he asked the question she was dreading. "Do you drink alcohol, Alice?" She nodded her head, but could not look him in the eyes. In a very quiet voice, almost a whisper, she told him truthfully, how her alcohol intake had increased substantially over the past few months. Alice asked if he was willing to tell her the exact results of her liver function blood test. He explained the liver enzymes ALT and AST were raised three times above the normal limit. Alice gasped! She had no one to blame but herself. She was the one who had drunk herself into a stupor which had resulted in her recent diagnosis of pneumonia. The doctor smiled kindly at Alice, he reassured her that no one was here to judge her, they were here to aid her recovery. He also advised her that she was slightly iron deficient and needed a short course of iron to build up her depleted iron stores. In addition, he advised Alice that the only route to the recovery of her liver was to abstain from alcohol, and if she was in agreement they could refer her to the drug and alcohol team for counselling. Alice was horrified at the idea of visiting a drug and alcohol team. The number of times she herself had referred patients to the local clinic, she never imagined that one day she would be a client herself. Their conversation was interrupted when Nurse Monroe arrived with her next dose of antibiotics. He told her this would be the last dose of intravenous antibiotics as tomorrow her cannula would be removed and she was to be commenced on oral medication. He asked Alice if she would like to freshen up.

She glanced at the disgusting hospital gown with half the ties missing, creating gaps at the back.

Oh Alice, Alice where have you gone? she thought to herself. What a fright she must look! She lifted her free hand to run it through her hair. Nurse Monroe felt her pain. He told her that his shift ended in two hours, but was on early the next morning when he planned to wheel Alice to the shower room so she could wash her hair, which he thought must be quite lovely. Meanwhile he offered to fetch her a bowl and that perhaps with her free hand she could freshen herself. The nurse had no sooner removed the wash bowl and towel when she saw a familiar face in the crowd of people making their way through the ward doors.

It was visiting time and Sally was now making headway towards her. Although they had only briefly met that day on *Poppy*, Alice felt a connection with Sally that she could not explain.

Alice knew that it was likely Sally had saved her life. If she had not arrived home from the Netherlands earlier than expected, who knows what would have happened? It was highly likely that she would have died, if not from pneumonia then hypothermia and dehydration. Who knows?

Sally was shocked at the change in Alice, she looked so tiny and frail, and her skin was sallow verging on jaundiced. She felt a familiar pain in her heart. The memories of her own son came flooding back. The years of heartache and worry, the many futile visits to the hospital to help him recover from the street drugs he continued to pump into his frail body. Sally had failed her son, but she was not going to fail Alice. At first, Alice was a little shy with Sally, mostly due to the contempt she held herself in and her shame. She could not find the right words to say. However, Sally made it easy for her. She did all of the talking. For she knew how therapeutic it had been for her. The past five years had taught Sally that with the right support and the passing of time, heartache, although never completely disappears, becomes manageable and easier to deal with. Deep in the corner of her heart, was a void that could never be filled. Sometimes the pain surfaced. Seeing Alice so frail and ill had triggered such a reaction on the day of her return when she found Alice slumped on the bow of the boat, her clothes wet with urine and vomit. She had recoiled at the sight of this lovely lady who had opened her heart to her on the day she left for her secondment, working in a drug and alcohol centre in Venlo. Sally had agreed to work as an observer in the Netherlands to learn about the care and support provided to their own unfortunate drug and alcohol dependent patients. Sally knew that Alice was deeply troubled, but was unaware of her alcohol dependence. Alice, evidently, had hidden this well. Had Sally known this before, she questioned herself about whether she would have rented the boat to her. The answer was yes she would.

Alice had needed a sanctuary and *Poppy* had played a part in providing that.

The rest was Alice's own responsibility. Sally promised that she would not berate herself for failing to notice that Alice was potentially an alcoholic. For that matter, it was likely that Alice hadn't recognised it in herself.

Denial is a major issue in drug and alcohol abuse, this much she had learned early on, when her son Zak had succumbed to the evils of street drugs at the tender age of thirteen. Encouraged by his so-called friends, he accepted his first cannabis infused cigarette behind the bike sheds. The first of many, Sally had been totally unaware of Zak's early use of drugs. However, later when she reflected, she remembered how Zak had developed mood swings, sometimes severe. It was pure ignorance on her part, for at the time she associated the changes in Zak as being part of adolescence and his rising testosterone levels. How wrong she had been. By the time Sally was aware, Zak was cannabis dependent and already showing early symptoms of paranoia. It was only by chance that she found out at all. Apparently, some of his school friends had been chatting about Zak on the school bus. They had spoken of him as a cool guy, a non-conformist to the chains of parents and society. He was described as being heavily into drugs and the man to go to for your own supply. That day however, was the day that the usual bus driver was off sick and the temporary driver was the husband of one of Sally's friends. It was a month later before her friend Angela summoned the courage to inform Sally. That day was the beginning of a living hell for her. A nightmare that was never ending until that final day. At first, she was in denial: there must have been some mistake, the boys were telling lies, causing trouble.

It was a mistake. Not her Zak, who was her world, her precious son. He was such a fun loving, loyal boy, never any trouble to her as a child. His thoughtful ways had melted her heart on many occasions. His school reports told of a young man who was bright and intelligent. His talents lay in the art and music subjects and this came as no surprise to Sally. She had struggled and scrapped to give him a good life, mostly to compensate for the lack of a father figure. Zak's father had abandoned Sally the moment the two positive blue lines appeared on the pregnancy test. He told Sally to count him out on this one, she was on her own. Sally was in the final year of her sociology degree and thought herself in love. Ethan was an art student. He captured her heart, that was for certain. He described himself as a free spirit. He freed himself alright, right out of Sally and Zac's life. He had never seen his son. Sally chose not to take the easy way out as many other young women of her time did. Abortion was not an option for her. From the moment she knew of her pregnancy, of the new life growing inside of her, she loved that life of her own flesh and blood. And loved him she had, through good times and bad. By the time Zak was eighteen he was injecting heroin into any vein he could. Three times he had entered a drug rehabilitation clinic and three times returned to his habit. Zak tried hard to stay clean, and suffered in the process. More than anything he wanted to make his mum proud, he loved her so much. More than anything. Anything except heroin. Zak suffered terribly for his addiction. He developed numerous injection site abscesses, causing horrific pain and disfigurement in his lower legs. The abscess wounds developed into deep venous and arterial leg ulcers requiring daily dressings. Sally was taught by the by the local community nurse team and the tissue viability nurse how to assess Zak's wounds and how to bathe and dress them with appropriate dressings. The wounds had leaked profusely, and needed many layers of dressings and bandages. He frequently needed antibiotics and analgesics, but still Zak managed to get out to his supplier and source more heroin. The methadone program had helped for a while and at times Sally had the occasional glimmer of hope for her son. These were very special times for her and Zak. These times were short lived and despite his horrific leg ulcers, Zak still managed to find a vein he could use. The pain in his legs was so intense that he needed to use increasingly higher doses of drugs, until that fateful day when he had taken more than his frail young body was able to cope with. The moment Sally saw two police officers at her door, she had that heart sinking feeling she had been expecting for years. Two police officers was not a good sign. With trepidation she invited them into her home, where with the greatest compassion they informed Sally of her son's death. They told Sally of the extremely sad squalid conditions in which Zak had been discovered.

Later: much later, after the inquest, the family liaison officer approached Sally, offering her support and encouraged her to seek out bereavement counselling. Sally was sign posted to various agencies, but it wasn't until after his funeral that she decided to engage with the Counselling Service.

Sally pulled up a chair and sat close to Alice at the side of her bed. She knew that Alice would be in denial and was unlikely at this stage to admit to herself or anyone else that she was an alcoholic. Her years spent working with drug and alcohol dependent clients had taught her very early in her career, that acknowledging there was a problem was the first step to a possible recovery. With this in mind Sally aimed her conversation primarily around the pneumonia diagnosis and not the root cause. Initially, Alice went along the same conversational path, although her recollection of the preceding events was somewhat limited.

Instead, she diversified by talking about *Poppy* and how much she had enjoyed staying on board. She emphasized how the boat had felt like a sanctuary and had given her an opportunity to reflect about the happy times she had spent with Robin, cruising on their own boat.

Sally listened with interest as Alice described the many places she had visited and the joy they had both shared. As Alice spoke about this part of her past, Sally noticed how her expression changed from a blank canvas to a face that lit up and shone, the tension momentary disappeared from her face. This is the true Alice, thought Sally.

"Does Robin or your family know that you are? In hospital?" Sally gently enquired. It was a few moments before Alice spoke. She told Sally it had been some weeks since she had last made contact and since then had mislaid her mobile phone which contained a list of contact numbers. "But your family must be so anxious about you, Alice. You have to contact them to put their minds at rest. Let them at least know where you are.

"Think about what you are putting them through. Surely your husband is concerned and your step children, they must be asking after you. You told me of how close your family are, you told me of your beautiful home and garden. A home you were once happy in. Please Alice, please make contact.

"I have been a victim of similar circumstances, waiting by the telephone for news of a loved one. Don't put people you love through such pain, I beg you. One day when you are stronger, I will explain how I know of that desperate, sinking feeling, when a loved one has disappeared." Sally handed Alice her own mobile phone. Alice did not have the energy to argue, neither did she have a clear head to memorise any of her family's mobile phone numbers. But she clearly remembered one land line number. A number ingrained in her head for so many years. With trembling hands, Alice pressed the keys to her mum's telephone. She heard the dialling code and planned her speech.

The phone was quickly answered and her mum's familiar voice was like food to a starving man. Alice took a deep breath into her weakened lungs and put on an Oscar winning performance.

She told her mum that she had lost her mobile phone and had been unwell for a short while, but she was now recovering and that more than anything, she was not to worry.

Apparently Alice was too late to deliver such a statement, for Robin and her children had reported Alice as missing and now it was in the hands of the police. The police were checking mobile phone records with a view to locating her whereabouts. Alice gasped! She pleaded with her mum, to contact her husband and children immediately. What had she done? How many lives had she affected with her weakness for alcohol? Her mother would surely be ashamed of her if she knew the truth. Alice explained that she was using a friend's phone and was unable to contact her husband and children without their numbers. She requested her mum write down the contact numbers for her and she would ring back in twenty minutes to retrieve them. Alice collapsed back on her pillow. The call had lasted only a matter of minutes, but had left her severely breathless and weak. Beads of sweat gathered on her forehead and her chest heaved up and down beneath the thin sheet. Sally noticed a water jug and glass on the bedside locker. She poured a small amount in the glass and told her that she would bring some cordial when she next visited.

Sally gently put the glass to Alice's lips. She sipped the water, but her lips were so dry and cracked it made little difference to her intense thirst. Alice lifted her free hand to touch her dry lips. In doing so, she caught sight of her hand. Her hand was grubby and scratched with broken jagged nails and torn cuticles. Her wrist was thin and there was a yellow tinge to her sagging skin. Sally gently held her hand. No words were spoken. Actions, not words, expressed the empathy from this remarkable woman. Alice knew that it had been a good day indeed, the day she met Sally. Alice was not a believer in fate or fantasy yet she had the feeling someone had sent Sally to be her guardian angel. Sally rummaged in her handbag and retrieved a pen and small notebook, she suggested Alice now contact her mum and for Alice to repeat the numbers as her mum read them out and Sally planned to write them down. True to her word, Alice's mum had the numbers ready. Her mum promised Alice that she would contact Robin and her children immediately to inform them that that Alice would be in touch before the day was out. A tall order for Alice, who was already exhausted and desperately needed to sleep. She needed time to prepare her story, to convince her children not to come post haste. She did not want them to see her like this. No way was that going to happen, but they needed reassurance as soon as possible and only her voice could do that. Nurse Monroe came to check on Alice. He needed to attend to her four hourly observations, her temperature was still not back to normal and was giving him concern. Sally excused herself and said that she would return shortly. Nurse Monroe checked the intravenous drip. The bag was collapsing in on itself, suggesting the antibiotics were nearly through. They had steadily been dripping into her veins since she had been admitted to the hospital. She enquired about her health status. Nurse Monroe smiled.

"I'm afraid your temperature is still a little raised, it will likely be a few more days before it is near normal. Alice we will also need to be sure that you have a suitable environment arranged for your convalescence as you will need help for a while yet. It is the hospital policy to check these details. I am sure you are aware of this." Alice sighed. What was she going to do? Where could she go to convalesce without her family knowing the truth? But she needn't have worried. Sally had arranged everything. Sally returned, bearing gifts from the voluntary shop. She placed a bottle of cordial on the bedside locker along with a basket of fruit. She winked at Alice.

"I know it's going to be difficult, but with my help and gentle persuasion, fruit smoothies will one day be your drink of choice," she grinned. Alice looked uncertain. She was craving a glass of brandy, a glass of anything alcoholic, come to think of it. The withdrawal symptoms were taking hold of her already, she wondered if anything could be prescribed to help her with the symptoms. Perhaps a small dose of diazepam.

At least she was in a safe environment, which is better than most people had under such circumstances. After all, there was nothing she could do at the moment, as she was tied to the bed with the cannula in the back of her hand. It was a Venflon, she knew how to remove it, after all, Alice had removed many in the past, but never from her own vein. Sally distracted her destructive thoughts. She pulled out another bag from inside of her own tote bag. Out of the bag Sally retrieved a pretty cotton night shirt and a pair of slippers for Alice. She was very grateful, and thought how wonderful and kind Sally was, but how could she walk out of the ward in these clothes? She could not escape in such garments. Alice tried to look pleased. Sally was no fool.

She guessed what was going through her friend's mind. She told Alice that her clothes were in such a terrible mess that everything she was wearing on the day of her admission, had been disposed of. However, with her permission, she would be happy to launder the dirty clothes that Alice had left on the boat and also bring some fresh clothes in readiness for her discharge. What Sally conveniently forgot to mention, was that it would take her a day or two to get the clothes laundered, meanwhile Alice was going nowhere. Alice gently nodded her head and once again thanked Sally for her kindness. She was feeling so sleepy and could hardly keep her eyes open. Sally acknowledged this and wished Alice good night. She left her mobile phone and the notebook on the locker. Before leaving the ward, she called into the sisters' office and told them of her plans to return the following day. She also informed them that she had a home for Alice and was happy to take care of her for however long was necessary.

She gave them a brief history of her experience as a social worker and her work with the drug and alcohol team. All that was required now was to convince Alice; that would be the greatest challenge. She knew from experience how dependence on drugs and alcohol changed people's personalities and how their values and beliefs were eroded away. She realised that Alice may be unpredictable, that she might try any method to obtain an alcohol fix.

The sound of a rattling trolley disturbed Alice from a very deep sleep. For a second she was confused as to where she was. A cheery voice welcomed her back to reality.

"Fancy a cuppa, luv?" The kitchen domestic looks impatient and sounded a little aggressive, thought Alice. She deduced that the domestic was probably running late and still had lots to do. Alice shook her head. She was tempted to ask for something stronger, but she could see it would fall on deaf ears and the domestic was not in good humour. Alice asked if she could pass her a drink of water, she was rewarded with nothing more than a scowl. Likely too much effort for her, thought Alice, so she attempted to reach the glass of water herself. It was more difficult than she had anticipated and in the process, knocked the glass, which went crashing to the floor, drawing the attention of a young nurse who was assisting another patient. The nurse smiled and made her way over to Alice.

"Let me help you," she said.

The young nurse looked to be about nineteen years of age, she was very slim and attractive and exuded enthusiasm. The same excited enthusiasm Alice had felt as a young student nurse. "Oh dear, some of the water has splashed onto the notebook," she said. That got the attention of Alice.

"What time is it please, Nurse?" she enquired.

"Just gone nine o'clock," she replied. Alice knew it was time to ring Mathew, he would be home from work now. Mathew was very astute and not easily fooled.

He also had a background in medicine. She would not be able to pull the wool over his eyes. Alice asked the nurse if she would mind passing her the mobile phone and notebook. She rang her son. The relief in his voice was evident, so much so, that she felt her heart melt.

Mathew told Alice of his conversation with her mum but she had been vague as to what was medically wrong. Alice told him that she had deliberately avoided telling her mum the details, in order to spare her worry. Alice wasn't entirely truthful with Mathew either. Alice informed him of the pneumonia diagnosis and as a result had needed to be hospitalised. He questioned his mum about the diagnosis, so feeling pushed into a corner, she had to mislead him by saying that the pneumonia was a complication following a recent bout of influenza. This seemed to placate him. However, what she failed to tell him was her abnormal liver function tests and anaemia. Alice was not ready to fall off the pedestal her son had placed her on many years ago.

Alice decided that to tell lies or omit the truth for the greater good was the kindest thing to do.

As a young man, Mathew admired his mum's strong character and work ethos. One of his favourite quotes from mum was about deferred gratification, something he had long practised.

Mathew enquired as to what his mum had been doing for the last few months? Alice told Mathew that she had needed a change of scenery. A place of solace where she could return to her previous state of physical and mental wellbeing. In doing so she had met Sally, who owned a canal boat and that she had sort of been boat sitting. She told Mathew that it was a mutual arrangement. Sally needed someone to take care of the boat and Alice had needed a place to stay, where she could relax, read, write and recover. She told Mathew about how delightful *Poppy* was and that the boat was moored around Camden Lock, an area that Mathew was also familiar with. Alice explained that was when she had taken ill. Sally had fortunately returned home early and made arrangements for her to go to the hospital. Somewhat true, thought Alice.

Mathew listened patiently, but he was not convinced. She was the kindest and most generous person he had ever known and had taught him so many valuable lessons in life. She had encouraged him with his studies, they had often studied together when his mum was doing her degree. Mother and son, like peas in a pod. He was well aware of how difficult his mum's life had become at home, but he always imagined that she could rise above the problems with the support of Robin, but now he realised that had been his naïve mistake. Robin had let his mum down, and he had been too short sighted to see it. While he understood her need to escape for rest and rehabilitation. It was out of character for his mum. There had to be more to it, and there was only one way to find out.

"Mum, which hospital are you in?" he enquired. She told him the name of the hospital and the ward number. "I am coming over tomorrow," he said. "I will be there mid-afternoon and collect Anne Marie on my way over. You need your family with you, and I won't take no for an answer." He told his mum that he loved her and wished her a good night's sleep.

Tomorrow afternoon, thought Alice. Her feelings were mixed. The idea of seeing her children filled Alice with joy and yet how could she let them see her like this? Alice tossed and turned in the bed, she was unable to get comfortable, she felt hot and anxious, her pulse was racing and the beginning of a headache was lurking just behind her eyes.

The young nurse who had helped earlier came over to Alice and enquired if she was alright. Alice asked if she could have two paracetamol when the evening medication was being issued. The nurse said of course, and she would also be back later to empty her catheter bag. "What?" said a startled Alice. It had never occurred to her, that not once had she needed to ask for the toilet and considering that it was likely she had been given three litres of intravenous fluids up to date, she really should not have been surprised.

Things were even worse than expected. Alice felt under the bed clothes. Sure enough she was catheterized. How embarrassing. Alice understood the procedure, she didn't need to ask the reason why. She already knew. Full of shame and embarrassment, Alice hid herself way down under the covers, the more she thought about it, and the more she felt irritation from the catheter.

She felt like tugging it and pulling it out. She needed to get a grip. Common sense prevailed. She knew what trauma could occur from pulling out the catheter with the internal balloon inflated.

The whole idea was absurd. What was wrong with her? She became aware of a trickling sound, and saw the nurse emptying her catheter bag. She told Alice that her output was good and if this continued, the catheter would be removed tomorrow.

"And my cannula?" asked Alice.

"Yes, that too," smiled the nurse. "Now can I get you a warm milky drink, to help you sleep?"

Surprisingly, she enjoyed the milk, and knowing the catheter and cannula would be removed before her children visited, put her mind somewhat at peace. In another life, thought Alice, I will make milk my tipple of choice. The lights were dimmed around ten o'clock as was the ward protocol. But Alice could not find sleep. This did not go unnoticed as the two nurses did the two o'clock drug round. They offered her another milky drink and ask if she wanted some company.

Alice accepted the drink, she wasn't in the humour for company but understood what a long shift it could be, while on night duty, so she nodded politely. She introduced herself as Nurse Lomax.

She was older than Alice had thought, at twenty-three she had already been a qualified nurse for two years. And was enjoying her work very much. Alice told Nurse Lomax that until recently she had worked in primary care and previously had worked twenty years at the hospital. They swapped stories of their training years and spoke of how things had changed in the NHS.

Although old school, Alice remarked that in her honest opinion the NHS had gone from strength to strength.

She herself valued the changes that had taken place. The advancement in medicine and surgery was a credit to the country. Alice described herself as being very patriotic and proud of the NHS. Nurse Lomax looked kindly at Alice. She had read her admission notes and seen the blood results, but this was not the right time to discuss it. Whatever had happened to Alice was repairable. She needed the right support and lots of love. No doubt that fundamentally she was a strong and determined lady, Nurse Lomax had a good feeling that things would turn out just fine. Alice needed to sleep, but there was something on her mind. Something she needed to ask Nurse Lomax.

Sure enough, as promised, Nurse Lomax removed the catheter and cannula before going off duty. She also wrote something very important in Alice's ward record. It had been playing on Alice's mind and Nurse Lomax had put that at rest. As instructed by Alice, she had written that, at Alice's request, no one was to be told of her abnormal liver tests or her alcohol dependence.

Only the pneumonia could be revealed, if any of her family enquired. Alice understood confidentiality, but the reassurance that this information had been highlighted put her mind at peace. When her children came to visit, it would be one less worry. Following the shift hand over from night staff to day staff the ward was buzzing with activity. Alice was offered breakfast. She managed a small dish of cereal and a glass of juice. The tea was disgusting and she knew the staff would be far too busy to prepare her some mint tea, so Alice lay back in bed and reminisced about her own time on the wards. She knew the staff would be organising the patients' hygiene needs. She was desperate to have a shower, she had been sweating so much, and her own body smell repulsed her.

The odour from her skin was made worse by the high dose of antibiotics she had been given to fight the infection. This was an odour she recognized from her work on the medical wards. Nurse Monroe called good morning, to Alice. She waved him over.

"I hear you have had your cannula and catheter removed," he said. "The night staff also reported that your temperature is improving, so how are you feeling this morning Alice?" Alice forced a smile.

She said that she felt marginally better although very uncomfortable and was desperate for a shower. She asked if Nurse Monroe had the time to assist her before breakfast as she felt it would be beneficial and help her appetite. "Besides," she smiled. "If I am clean and sat out of bed, the food should taste more appetising, don't you think?"

He looked towards the other staff who had congregated around the breakfast trolley. He beckoned Alice to swing her legs over the edge of the bed. With difficulty she manoeuvred her body towards the edge. Pure steely motivation helped her overcome the weakness in her back as she sat upright. Nurse Monroe helped to put on the slippers that Sally had kindly bought her the previous day. He reached into the locker and retrieved the new night shirt. Holding Alice's hands, he eased her off the bed. Her legs felt very shaky and weak. It took a moment to get her balance. He motioned towards the ward entrance.

"It's not far, Alice, I will hang on to you, don't worry. I will find you a clean towel and some toiletries. We have quite a good supply donated by a local charity. I believe there are a few new combs as well, and looking at your unruly mane I suspect that you will need one," he laughed. Alice was not at all offended, she rather liked Nurse Monroe. Slowly and steadily, she made her way to the shower room. Her hospital gown, flapping open behind her, revealing her thin, sickly body. How undignified she felt. Nurse Monroe provided her with the towel and toiletries as promised. He showed her the emergency pull chord in case of difficulty and left Alice to enjoy the shower in peace.

The shower felt oh so good. Alice scrubbed her body clean, she washed her hair three times to remove the smell of sweat and vomit. At last she felt a little piece of her dignity return. Clean body, clean mind, she thought. Rubbing herself dry, she noticed the slight yellow tinge to her skin was improving and less noticeable. With luck, her children would not notice at all. Her skin though, was in poor condition and very dry. Thankfully she had no bruising.

Having put on her nightgown and slippers, she pulled the chord for assistance back to her bedside chair.

Her mouth felt dry and dirty, in dire need of mouthwash, but it was doubtful Nurse Monroe would be able to provide such luxuries. Perhaps Sally would be kind enough to go to the voluntary shop for her. Alice knew that she owed Sally a great debt on many levels, not only in terms of saving her life, but also she owed her money. Alice hated owing money and always felt the need to urgently pay her debts. This would be her main priority at the first opportunity.

Nurse Monroe was busy attending to another patient, so she was assisted to her chair by a student nurse. She pulled a table alongside Alice and offered breakfast. Having just witnessed the dreadful state of her skin and her declining muscle mass, she agreed to a small bowl of porridge and a glass of milk. Alice knew this was a small step on a long journey to her recovery, but she needed to start somewhere. After breakfast, she had nothing else to do except watch the comings and goings on the ward. The staff were all working extremely hard, helping patients with their hygiene, stripping many beds and carrying out medical procedures. The ward domestics were scurrying around with dusters and mops, vacuum cleaners and antiseptics. The ward was a hive of activity. At ten o'clock, Alice was given her first dose of oral antibiotics.

Following this, the phlebotomist came and obtained a sample of her blood, to review her liver function test and full blood count to see if the anaemia was improving. Mid-morning, Nurse Monroe took Alice to the radiography department for a repeat chest x-ray, to see if the pneumonia was resolving. In fact, she was feeling a little less short of breath, and the steamy shower had helped her to expectorate a large amount of mucus from her lungs. She felt less congested, so hopefully the x-ray would give a positive result. Alice felt a little cold as she was being wheeled down the long corridor to the radiography department. The thin blue hospital blanket which contained more cotton than wool, was very ineffective in terms of warmth, however, it did cover her now skinny legs and provided her with some dignity. The radiographer checked her details and performed the procedure. Nurse Monroe informed Alice that they would need to wait around for the results in case the x-ray needed repeating. She had anticipated this.

Alice said she didn't mind at all and was happy to be left if Nurse Monroe wanted a coffee break. But he would hear nothing of the sort and told Alice he intended to stay with her. They chatted about the news and current affairs at first. Then Alice deliberately changed the subject. She briefly told him of her own career in nursing and how circumstances had led her into her current situation. He listened with interest. Then he surprised her when he said that she was ideally placed to help others who may find themselves in a similar situation. He reinforced the idea by citing her qualifications and her life experiences as perfect for a role in social care. Alice thanked him for his belief in her, but at this current moment in time, her goal was to lose the chains of alcohol dependence that were dragging her down, worse than any chattels ever invented. A dependence on alcohol and, what she had now began to realise, a deep and slow depression that had culminated over a long time. It must have crept up on her, slowly and surely changing her perspective and eroding away the true Alice.

The chest x-ray did not need repeating and Alice was returned to the ward in time for lunch.

The whole ward routine appeared to be centred on meal times and consultant rounds, thought Alice. She managed a small amount of thin soup, followed by a fruit yogurt. Alice knew the large amount of antibiotics she had been administered would play havoc with her gut and she would likely develop thrush symptoms within the next few days. She made a mental note to accept the yogurts on a regular basis. The probiotics, although in small amounts, were going to be beneficial. Visiting time was approaching. Alice began to plan her conversation with Mathew and Anne Marie. She ached to see them and wished with all of her heart that the meeting was under different circumstances. But this was what it was and she had to make the best of it. As it turned out, she was once again helped by Sally, who seemed to be her guardian angel. Sally was the first visitor to arrive. She could not be missed, walking down the ward with her bright flamboyant clothes and long chestnut hair, tied with a brightly coloured scarf. Quite the bohemian, thought Alice and she remembered how Anne Marie had long ago thought the same of herself. Sally came bouncing towards Alice, with a big smile on her face.

"I have a proposition for you, Alice. Please hear me out before you give your answer." She told Alice that she had some annual leave owed to her from work. And in addition, she had some dedicated study time to write up her report on the studies she had made in the Netherlands while observing the way the Dutch supported their own drug and alcohol patients. In total, Sally had eight weeks in which she would very much like to travel along the Grand Union canal. Sally explained that it would help her enormously if she had a capable crew member who knew how to handle the boat, and the locks and who better than Alice? They could help each other. She hoped the fresh air and the tranquillity of the countryside would help Alice with her convalescence. Alice saw the excitement in her friend's face and knew it was a smoke screen in order to help her recover.

How could she refuse, after everything Sally had done for her? So it was agreed that, upon discharge from the hospital, they would journey together on the inland waterways.

"Mum, Mum!" Alice recognised that beautiful familiar voice of Anne Marie. A voice that her Mum could not tell apart from her own daughter, for when Anne Marie phoned her Gran, she sounded so much like Alice. Mathew and his sister came running towards their mum, arms stretched open wide and tears streaming down their young, anguished faces. No words were spoken as together they hugged their mum. Sally looked on in wonder. How fortunate Alice was, to have her children with her and it was clear how much they loved their mum. The pain she felt in her heart, was not of jealousy, but of longing beyond any measure for her own son Zak, she felt a deep need for him to wrap his arms around her and call her mum. Sally watched Mathew embrace his mum until finally he pulled away and looked questioningly at her. Alice introduced her children to Sally and explained that it was her boat she had been living on when she had taken ill. Alice went on to explain that she owed her life to Sally, who had returned early from her work in the Netherlands and had called the emergency services to her assistance. Sally soon realised they were not aware of the full story and knew better than to divulge any confidentialities that Alice preferred to keep to herself. Sally was about to excuse herself to allow the family some private time together, when Alice told the children of Sally's plans in terms of helping her to recover from the pneumonia. The relief on Anne Marie's face was plain to see and Mathew's too.

Mathew took something from his trouser pocket and handed it to his mum. It was a pay-as-you-go mobile phone.

He had put £50 credit on and requested that his mum phone at least every other day to either himself or his sister. He had entered only three numbers into the phone book. His own, his sister's and his Gran's. Alice thanked him, promising she would keep in touch. Sally listened with interest as they told their mum of their current job situations and the exciting lives they were leading. It was hard for Sally to bear. She bid them all farewell and handed Alice a tooth brush and toothpaste. Sally looked kindly at Alice and said she would visit the following day. Anne Marie noticed how thin and sallow-looking her mother had become. She was saddened by her mum's appearance. She had brought with her a vanity case containing indulgent toiletries and hair products for her mum and she immediately set to work, first giving her mum a pedicure and manicure then brushing her hair until it shone. Anne Marie then arranged it, high up on her head, making large curls which she gripped underneath leaving little tendrils of hair to frame her mum's face. Next she applied moisturiser to her mum's very dry and unhealthy looking skin. It was heart breaking for Anne Marie. It wasn't so long ago that her mum was radiant and full of vitality. She applied a little foundation and blush to her mum's hollow cheeks. A touch of lipstick finally managed to add a little colour to her mum's drawn face.

"Mum, you are beautiful and kind, we all miss you so much, we know you are not being honest with us about everything, we respect your privacy. We can also see that Sally is very sincere in her desire to help you recover. You are not alone, together we will support you and watch as you go from strength to strength," said Anne Marie. Alice began to cry, the first tears she had ever allowed her children to see. She was unable to hold them back, the tears somehow released the tight ball of wound up tension that had been trapped inside her body for a long time, a tension that was like a coiled up spring coiled tightly to the point of destruction.

As the tears fell and the emotion relaxed, Alice felt a glimmer of hope. She knew it was going to be a tough battle, but she was ready for the fight.

Mathew had disappeared to the voluntary shop while his sister was giving her mum a pampering session. He said he was popping to fetch his mum some mouthwash, but in truth it was an excuse to call in to the sister's office to check up on his mum's progress.

Sister Stanley opened the case notes of Alice and noted the special request of confidentiality. She spoke kindly to Mathew explaining his mum's pneumonia diagnosis and how she was slowly recovering. Mathew was sceptical and enquired if there was anything else he should know.

Sister Stanley advised him to speak with his mum about any other issues with respect to her long term health. Mathew said thank you, although the encounter was not as productive as he had hoped it would be. He accepted what he was told and on his return to his mum, he did not mention his chat in the sister's office. Her children remained with Alice until visiting time was over, when with a heavy heart she hugged them both and told them how much she loved them and wished them a safe journey. Emotionally and physically she was drained and welcomed sleep when it came. Alice was woken by Nurse Lomax who had arrived for her ten-hour night shift. Alice had slept right through supper and had missed her evening medication. It was still in the little plastic pot on the bedside locker. Nurse Lomax passed Alice a drink of water to take with her medication. She thanked her for the help and asked if she might have something to eat.

Nurse Lomax smiled and said, "That is a very good sign indeed." She was only too happy to provide Alice with a pack of sandwiches which had been left over from supper. The sandwiches tasted so good and the tea like nectar. It occurred to Alice that she had not thought about alcohol all day. Seeing her children and the comfort she had gained from their visit appeared to be a tonic in itself and her long deep sleep had reinforced her energy and cleared her head.

No longer did she feel weak of body and mind. The empty strange sensations in her body she had been enduring for the past few weeks were replaced with an enveloping awareness, almost a re-awakening of her soul. A soul that had been determined to stay within the framework of her weak and troubled body. A little spark of the old Alice was still alive within her and she hoped that with time, this small spark would once again burn into a flame of hope, passion and love.

She vowed to herself that above all else she would be the heroine of her own life and not the victim. She had come so close to losing the respect of those she loved. Alice thought of Robin and the rich history of shared memories, joy and sadness. Mathew had given her a mobile phone; she should ring Robin. But what would she say? Alice looked at the ward clock. It was ten thirty. Robin would be settled in front of the television by now, perhaps this was a good time to call.

Now her mind was not muddled with alcohol, she clearly remembered her home number. She heard the dial tone and began to think that no one would answer. Just before it clicked over to the answer phone, she heard a familiar voice. Her heart sank, she was hoping that Robin would answer. It was Stephen who answered the phone. Trying not to show the disappointment in her voice, she said hello, and asked how he was. Stephen sounded very drunk, making her recoil at the thought of how bad she must have sounded to the strangers she had spoken to as she drunkenly walked along the towpath. Stephen didn't seem surprised to hear from her, neither did he sound pleased. He told her that his father was out at the local pub, which is what he had done most nights since Alice had disappeared. What had she expected? Certainly not a welcome committee. The conversation was short, she said goodbye and that she would try to contact Robin again, but maybe a little earlier next time. Alice switched off the phone. It was getting late and would not be fair to the other patients if her phone was to ring, although she doubted very much that Robin would return her call.

The following morning she was feeling very much improved. Nurse Monroe was on the day shift and he told Alice that her temperature had been within normal limits for the past twelve hours.

Her oxygen saturation level was at 98% and her chest x-ray reported as satisfactory. Around midday, the consultant did his ward round. With his team around him he explained to the junior house officer about Alice's diagnosis. She hung her head in shame as he told them of her abnormal liver blood tests and the reason the liver was affected. The consultant examined Alice's chest and enquired if she would allow the junior doctors to sound her chest as part of their ongoing education. Meekly she nodded her head. After the examination they discussed their findings and it was agreed that her chest was more or less clear with only a slight crackle on the left lung base. He said that her latest liver test was improving which suggested signs of her liver recovering and, provided that she stayed off the alcohol, there was every reason to believe that her liver would make a full recovery. He then told her that she was suitable for discharge the following day and was to continue on the antibiotics for a further week. Immediately after the consultant left her bedside, she switched on her mobile phone. She was surprised to see on the history, six missed calls, all from her home landline. Alice looked at the time, it was two o'clock.

Robin would still be at work; she couldn't ring him there. But she did ring her mum and children to share the good news of her impending discharge. She told her mum of her children's visit and how it had been better than any medicine. When her mum enquired as to her future plans, Alice explained that for now she had no immediate long term plans but her short term plan in terms of her convalescence was to travel the inland waterways with her new found friend and saviour, Sally. Finally, her mum enquired if she was alright financially, now that she was no longer working. This truly hit a nerve with her, for with everything else happening she had forgotten about her diminishing bank balance. Alice thanked her mum for being so thoughtful and then asked her a huge favour.

"Mum, I know it is a big ask, and normally it would not be necessary but could you transfer some money into my account, just as a temporary measure? For now I prefer not to ask Robin, and I promise most sincerely I will pay you back every penny as soon as possible." Her mum was delighted to be helping her daughter, she did not hesitate. It was agreed that Alice would contact her mum the following afternoon with the bank account and sort code details. She explained that her details were on the boat and she hoped to be back on board the following day.

CHAPTER TEN

After finding Alice semi-conscious on the front of her boat, Sally was afraid of what she would find inside her lovely home. She really did not know what to expect, all kinds of scenarios past through her mind. Had Alice been entertaining other people on board? Had she been mugged, had the boat been burgled? But despite the condition of Alice, the boat had been well cared for.

It was not until she had ensured that Alice was in safe hands at the hospital, that Sally had discovered that all was fine at home. When she boarded the boat, the only things out of place were a dirty cup on the sink and the unmade bed. Otherwise, all was well. It appeared that Alice had done very little cooking and even less laundry, looking at the laundry basket which was half full. No wonder Alice was so thin and malnourished, poor thing, how she must have struggled on a daily basis, thought Sally. She gathered the clothes from the laundry basket and along with her own unpacked dirty clothes put them in a large, soft laundry bag. She then proceeded to strip the bed, collected the damp towels from the bathroom and made her way to the launderette.

By the following day, her boat was spick and span, the laundry done and the cupboards full of food. Any remaining alcohol on board, she poured down the sink.

Lucky fish, thought Sally. She replaced the alcohol with a selection of healthy nutritious juices. In addition she purchased: folic acid tablets, thiamine, vitamin B compound, milk thistle and multivitamins. Sally planned to take good care of Alice. But would she be receptive? Would Alice accept her help willingly with the true intention it was meant? She had tried so hard with Zak, he wanted to be helped, wanted to be healed and knew his mum wanted those things too, yet still it hadn't been enough.

When Sally visited Alice that evening she was so relieved to observe the change in her.

She certainly looked in better health, but looks could be deceiving and she knew from her experience with Zak, that remissions often gave false hope. Delighted to hear of her proposed discharge, Sally couldn't wait to talk about their future journey along the Grand Union Canal. She informed Alice that all the supplies were on board and other than fresh produce which they could purchase along the way, everything was more or less set. There was enough diesel in the tank to keep them moving for about one week, thereafter they could purchase more diesel along the route either from a marina or a travelling diesel and coal merchant. Sally had also stocked up on bags of coal and logs, to keep them warm in the evenings. Alice smiled. Many times she and Robin had spoken of travelling to London north to south along the Grand Union Canal. But this she never expected. Alice thanked the day that she had seen the advertisement in the launderette.

How fortunate she had been to meet such a kind and compassionate friend like Sally. She knew very little about Sally's past, but she trusted her own judgement and at that first meeting knew instinctively that Sally was intrinsically a good person, someone who she could trust.

Sally chatted a while, mostly discussing Alice's life history. She enquired if Alice had contacted her mum, now that she had a mobile phone. Alice confirmed that she had, but she didn't mention her financial issues or the loan. However, she did ask Sally if she would search through her belongings for her debit card which was in the back of her purse. Sally agreed and enquired which clothes to bring for her journey out of the hospital. The weight loss had been dramatic since her illness and Alice needed to consider which of her clothes would be suitable, or even clean. But she need not have worried, Sally said that she had a full bag of clean clothes and would bring the lot, so Alice could choose. It was gone eight when Sally left. Anxiously, Sally turned on her mobile phone and once again rang home. This time Robin did answer.

The relief in his voice was clear to Alice. He explained that he had arrived home late on the evening she had rang. He went on to explain that Stephen was asleep on the sofa when he entered the lounge, but on waking, the very first thing he said was that you had finally made contact. It was a good five minutes before Alice could get a word in. Robin was so full of questions, he hardly gave her chance to answer, before he directed another enquiring question to her. He told her how along with Mathew and Anne Marie he had gone to the police to report her missing, such was his worry. Alice took a moment to compose herself, she needed to try and let go of the tangle of negative feelings that were slowly building up inside of her as she thought about the roots of her problem. Since being in hospital, she had come to realise that she had been through a long and painful process that had started with the breakdown of her first marriage and gathered pace with the problems she had encountered with Robin and his family. She took a deep and steady breath to compose herself. Alice did not want this encounter with Robin to go badly. He was suffering too, Robin had his own past pain to deal with and she did not wish to reinforce this pain any further. Calmly Alice explained how she had met Sally, who was willing to rent her boat while away in the Netherlands on a work placement. Alice knew that Robin would be interested in the details of the boat, so she told him about *Poppy* and the area the boat was moored in London. For a while they reminisced of the happy times they had spent together on their own boat, a subject they were comfortably able to discuss without any remorse. No mention was made of the reasons as to why she had disappeared, Robin was just happy to know that Alice was safe. She told him that she had been taken ill with pneumonia and was currently in hospital, but was now well enough to be discharged.

Robin was saddened to hear that his wife had been so ill and he wasn't able to be there for her. When he enquired as to why she had taken so long to make contact, Alice lied to him.

She was so ashamed of the truth and how she berated herself for the catastrophic errors of judgement that she had made. Alice enquired about her step children and how things were at home. Robin was reluctant to say very much and Alice saw this as a red flag, so she didn't pursue the issue. Nurse Lomax appeared at the bedside with the offer of a milky drink, advising that soon the ward lights were to be dimmed. Actually, Alice was quite relieved. It gave her the opportunity to close the conversation with Robin. She told Robin that she was so very sorry if she had caused him pain. She told him that she loved him and thought about him often. Robin said goodnight. He did not return the sentiment.

When Sally came the following day, she handed Alice the bank card as requested. She also passed her a large bag containing the fresh laundered clothes as promised. Alice thanked Sally and asked if she minded being left a moment while she went to shower and change. Sally told Alice that she would go to the hospital voluntary shop and have a coffee. When Sally left, Alice retrieved her mobile phone, the bank card and toiletries. Although large and heavy, she carried the bag of clothes to the shower room, where she promptly rang her mum and passed on the bank details. Following a short conversation with her mum, Alice checked out the contents of the bag. On opening the bag, a lovely fragrance of honeysuckle and jasmine filled the room. Tears began to form in the corners of her eyes; she felt very emotional. So many people were helping her. How could she possibly repay them? In terms of financial payment, Alice had every intention of paying back Sally the money she owed. In addition, she would share the expenses for the journey they had planned together. Her mum had told Alice that the money should be in her account within the next hour or two, which was of enormous help to her, for Alice knew that not only did she need to pay Sally, but in addition she also needed suitable clothes for working the locks. Ballerina shoes and Capri pants would be useless under such conditions.

She needed sturdy boots and a set of waterproof trousers and jacket at the very least. On her exit from the ward, Alice knocked on the sister's office door. She was pleased when Nurse Monroe answered the door. She thanked him for his kindness and requested if he would also pass her thanks to Nurse Lomax. He shook her hand and told Alice that he had every confidence in her recovery and that she must be very strong, for life was precious and he felt that she still had a lot to give. His words struck a chord with her. She thought about the other Alice, who was strong and brave when her marriage ended. A time when she had been determined to provide a good life for her children. Could she be that woman again? Time and the love of her family would be her salvation. Fate sent Sally, and although Alice had lived in one world and Sally in another, they had drifted towards one another, for reasons beyond her imagination. Sally and Alice called into the hospital pharmacy to collect her prescription, before heading out of the hospital. The fresh air in Alice's lungs felt unbelievably good. The coolness on her cheeks was like a wakeup call to life, she felt as though the last few days had belonged to someone else. Yes, she had been in a long bad dream. A nightmare that had drawn her down and down to the depths of despair, spiralling down into an abyss of alcohol induced behaviour.

The distance from the hospital to where *Poppy* was moored was quite a long way. Sally enquired if Alice was feeling strong enough to walk the distance. She told Sally that there was nothing she would like more. They walked together in relative silence. Conversation could wait.

For the moment, Alice was looking around her as though she had opened her eyes for the first time to the wonders of life and nature.

Walking along the towpath, they passed a group of young people sitting together on the grassy bank, drinking cans of lager. The familiar smell of alcohol breath and stale empty cans, triggered an unwelcome response.

She had been protected from these sensations in the clinical environment of the ward, but now she was back in the real world, where on a regular basis she could be tormented and tested. The demons in her head began playing tricks with her. She could almost taste the lager herself. The longing for an alcoholic drink was intense. Her body felt as though it had been taken over by some kind of outside force. She consciously tried to focus on walking forward and beyond the draw of alcohol. The smell of alcohol lingered in her senses long after they had passed by the group of young people. She had a terrible urge to run back to them and drink the dregs from the empty cans on the floor. Alice tensed her fingers and tightened her jaw. Her mind was telling her to have a drink of alcohol, as one small drink would satisfy the demons.

Sally had noticed the change in Alice's body language and the pained expression on her face.

She had seen this many times with Zak, who repeatedly succumbed to his demons... She took hold of Alice's hand and squeezed it reassuringly.

"It will soon pass," she calmly said. Sally knew that a good dose of distraction therapy would help Alice with this first hurdle. *Poppy* was the perfect distraction, and sure enough, just past the next bridge was *Poppy* in all of her magnificent welcoming glory. The reflection from the water shimmered along the blue paintwork of the hull. The bouquets of red poppies painted on each side of the boat cabin reminded Alice of the lives lost in war, young and old, fighting a cause they were passionate about. Alice was facing a different war, a war against alcohol dependence. Life was a gift; modern medicine had provided her with an opportunity to make a new start. She had been saved for a reason, unsure exactly what the reason was, and she had no idea. Alice locked away this thought at the back of her mind. Something she could use as a weapon against the cravings that would surely return.

Carefully she climbed down into the boat cabin. A delicious smell was coming from the kitchen.

The boat cabin was even cosier than she remembered. The stove was lit creating a warm relaxing atmosphere. New cushions were scattered on the sofa and a faux fur throw was laid across the arm. Sally beckoned Alice to the sofa and suggested she get some rest after the long and exhausting walk from the hospital. Alice did not argue, for Sally was absolutely right. She was tired and happily snuggled down on the sofa, covering herself with the warm soft throw.

She closed her eyes and listened to the gentle cracking of the fire. The smell of beef casserole drifted through the air. She knew that she was blessed and yet Alice was not at peace. She was scared.

Afraid of drifting back down into the abyss of depression and ultimately the grip of alcohol. She knew that thousands of tiny battles lay ahead of her. Alice considered the recent battle, that if not for Sally, she would have lost. She had felt life's terror and knew that was a place she never wanted to visit again. Alice began to analyse at what point her life had she started to spiral out of control. She tried to remember at what point in her life the old Alice had died. Was it the first time that Robin disregarded her feelings and put others before her, when she would have settled for equality? Surely not then. Was it when she had no alternative but to move out of her home to support Anne Marie because Robin did not come to her rescue? Or was it the day her daughter moved south to be with Andrew? It occurred to Alice that no single event had triggered her decline. She had a history of giving so much of herself and receiving so little in return. Alice knew that she was not without fault. She had contributed to her own decline. The truth was, no one was responsible for Alice, but Alice herself.

At some point she must have fallen asleep, for Sally was gently shaking her by the shoulders to rouse her from sleep in readiness to eat. She had set the table for supper and reminded Alice of the busy day ahead of them tomorrow. She encouraged her to eat as much as she could manage, to pack in the calories as much energy was required, something Alice was well aware of. After freshening up, she joined Sally at the table. The beef casserole was delicious, she praised Sally for her culinary skills and thanked her so very much for everything. Sally was full of anticipation for the journey ahead of them. The moment the supper pots were cleared off the table she unfolded a large inland waterways map on the table and with great excitement began to point out the route they would be taking. The plan was to travel as far as gas street basin in Birmingham, an area Alice was well familiar with. Alice was trying very hard to concentrate, but her mind constantly drifted into the past as she remembered planning similar journeys with Robin. Every day's journey culminated in finding a mooring spot either outside of a canal side inn or pub. If not outside, then certainly within walking distance. The memories of the pubs also triggered a craving for alcohol. How she longed for a glass of wine. She could almost taste the clear sharp taste of chardonnay. Her imagination went into overdrive, producing phantom whiffs of alcohol in the air around her. She began to fidget and became agitated. This did not go unnoticed by Sally, who knew only too well how difficult the next few days were going to be. Luckily, she was well prepared and knew exactly how to deal with the situation. But first, Sally needed to probe a little more about Alice's level of dependence on alcohol so that she could be of maximum assistance to her friend. Folding away the map, she distracted Alice from the tunnel that she was slipping in to.

She asked Sally if it was okay for her to make a mug of warm milk in the hope it would aid a restful sleep. After making the drink they moved to the sofa. Sally relaxed on the sofa cushions, tucking her legs beneath herself in the lotus position.

Alice sat rigid and tense, with her hands wrapped around the mug of warm milk like hugging a comfort blanket. She was tight of jaw and grinding her teeth together to try and displace the rising anxiety within her. Sally began to take slow deep breaths and encouraged

Alice to breathe with her at the same rate and rhythm. After a few minutes Alice felt less anxious, which was just as well, for Sally was ready to talk. Sally gently asked Alice about her historical drinking behaviour and also her recent drinking pattern. After much thought, Alice explained, in the past she was a very light drinker and when the children were small she abstained completely. She struggled to identify the exact point in time when her alcohol level increased, but she guessed that it was more than likely after her divorce. She realised that it had been a gradual process.

Nights out with her friends, and nights in with them, come to think about it. In addition, Robin enjoyed his beer and encouraged her to drink with him. Out of love and kindness he frequently bought her gifts of wine and occasionally spirits. She told Sally that her alcohol intake had increased with every family crisis and there had been plenty of them. Alice took a sip of her milk, for a moment or two she did not speak and then she told Sally that the tipping point for her, had been the moment she had moved out of the family home. Sally listened patiently, without interruption. She asked Alice if she considered herself dependent on alcohol in order to cope with life's difficulties. This time it took Alice a long time to answer Sally, as she had never said it out loud before, it took great courage for her to admit that she had a problem.

"I believe that I have a mildly dependent drinking problem which has and will, if not controlled, cause me serious harm," Alice quietly admitted. She told Sally, that of late, it hadn't mattered to her what she was drinking, provided it had dulled the desire for alcohol. Knowing that Alice had previously worked as a practice nurse and quite likely been involved with lifestyle counselling in relation to smoking, alcohol and drugs.

She enquired if Alice had any idea as to how many units of alcohol she had consumed on a daily basis. Alice did not answer. Realising that this was probably more than enough probing for one evening, Sally suggested they get settled for the night. She offered Alice the double bed, but Alice declined, telling Sally that she would be comfortable on the sofa and it was only right that Sally slept in her own bed. She thanked Sally for her consideration and bid her goodnight.

The following morning was all stations go. After breakfast, Sally disconnected the mains electric from the hook up and switched to battery. She put the tiller handle in position and secured it with a brass tiller pin. It was a cute brass duck. Sally started the engine. It roared into action, causing a vibration throughout the boat. She called to Alice, asking her to release the ropes securing the boat to the iron rings sunk in to the towpath. With trembling hands, Alice struggled to release the tight knots holding the boat secure. Eventually, she managed to free the knots and threw the thick black ropes onto the boat. There were three in all, at the bow, stern and centre.

The last rope to be released was the stern rope and she just managed to jump aboard as *Poppy* began to drift from the mooring. It was a cool and sunny morning, a few wisps of cloud promised to keep the day free of rain. Young commuters were cycling along the towpath making their way to work. Dog walkers, made their way briskly along the towpath, trying to avoid the cyclists.

Sally handled the boat well, Alice was content to sit on the locker and watch the morning life of London drift by as they made their way north. As the boat slowly and quietly travelled along the Grand Union Canal, they passed by a number of moored boats. Each time, Sally reduced the engine revs so has not to disturb the occupants or loosen their mooring ropes. Alice had always enjoyed checking out the unusual and often quirky names of the boats. If at all possible she would sneak a peep inside through the open hatch. On some of the boats were the engine was in the centre, the hatch was left open for the owner to proudly display a gleaming Lister engine and keep the cabin cool.

One such boat passed by them in the opposite direction, with the regular put-putting sounds and plumes of smoke coming out of the chimney. An elderly gentleman was at the stern. He tipped his hat towards Sally and herself. For a moment he reminded Alice of her father. At the very same moment, her heart skipped a beat. What would her beloved father have thought of her now?

She sincerely hoped that he was not looking down on her. She could not bear it. And her lovely mum and children. Alice was determined to get her life on track and she had every confidence that Sally would make sure of it. Towards midday the air was turning decidedly cooler. Alice began to shiver. She knew that she wasn't dressed appropriately for the weather and definitely did not have suitable clothes for working on a canal boat. She asked Sally if they might be mooring somewhere that she could purchase a pair of sturdy walking boots and waterproof clothing. Sally suggested they call in at the next marina chandlery, as she needed to purchase a spare calor gas canister. It was three hours later when they pulled into the marina and tied the boat up on the temporary moorings. Together they went to the chandlery. Alice knew that the money would now be in her account, so she purchased a pair of leather boots, waterproof jacket and trousers and a pair of leather gloves to protect her hands when handling the rough dirty ropes and operating the paddles on the locks. She also insisted on paying for the gas canister. A good start towards her share of the running costs. They had a short walk around the pretty marina. It was a very well established marina boasting a number of shops including a tea shop and bistro. Alice wondered if there was a cash machine on site as she was desperate to pay Sally the money that she owed. Alice hated being in debt to anyone and wouldn't rest until she had settled up with Sally. There was a nice bakery on site so Alice purchased a fresh crusty loaf of bread. While doing so, she enquired if there was a speed bank on site and was advised this facility was available at the main office.

Twenty minutes later they were back on the boat. Alice had managed to get the cash she needed and immediately handed Sally the money she owed for her last month's rent and a little extra to cover the purchases that Sally had kindly bought Alice while in hospital. While moored on the marina they had soup and the fresh bread. Before setting off, Sally told Alice, it was a good hour before the next lock, so perhaps during that time she could prepare a casserole in the slow cooker for the evening meal. She also suggested for Alice to set the wood burning stove ready to put a light to it later in the evening as it would likely turn cold. Alice was only too happy to be useful and was grateful for the opportunity to be inside the boat, as she was feeling the cold, much more than usual. Which wasn't a great surprise to her as she had very little flesh covering her bones. In addition, none of her clothes fitted properly and even though she had on extra layers, they didn't sit snug next to her body. Alice smiled to herself, remembering the fleecy lined liberty bodices her parents made her wear in the winter as a child. That is exactly what I need now, thought Alice. Setting the fire was very therapeutic for her. Laying the scrunched up paper and piling the sticks into a criss-cross stack, she placed a fire lighter beneath the stack and a few cobbles of coal on the top. She was satisfied that her work of art would provide them with a good roaring fire that evening. She envisaged the flames leaping up the chimney creating a warm glow in the salon of the boat. A thought crossed her mind. Many years previous, during a psychology lecture, she was taught of a technique to aid self-cleansing of the mind. The idea was to write down all of the troubles and demons that haunted a person's mind, then screw up the paper into a ball and bury it in the ground. Alice thought that it might help if she burned her demons.

Yes, that was what she would do. But first, Alice needed to prepare a chicken casserole. Sally had certainly stocked the cupboards well. She found fresh chicken thighs in the fridge, which she rolled in seasoned flour and fried in oil for a few minutes.

While the chicken was frying she chopped onions, garlic, mushrooms and peppers. She found a pot of fresh parsley growing in a small decorative plant pot. Alice took off a few leaves and along with some dried herbs de province chicken stock and further seasoning she put everything in the slow cooker and set to simmer. Normally at this stage Alice would add a good measure of wine. Red or white, whatever was left over from the previous evening drinking session. This thought once again reinforced her desire for an alcoholic drink. The urge was even stronger than the last time. Her lips felt parched and she could almost hear her own voice calling out for a drink. It was to no avail. Sally had made sure that there was not one single drop of alcohol on board, not even medicinal Indian brandy. She looked longingly at the wine glasses in the glass peninsular unit and hoped that just holding a glass in her hand with a tonic water in, might help to quell the demons. Surprisingly, it did help a little and she quite enjoyed the sharp slightly aromatic taste. So she poured another. Sally called from the back of the boat.

On the way to the back, Alice switched the inverter on to alter the power from twelve vaults to two hundred and forty vaults while the slow cooker was on. She joined

Sally who was guiding the tiller. They had been sailing five hours. She told Alice that there were good moorings on the other side of the lock. They decided it was time to relax for the evening, so after setting the lock and coming through the other side they decided to moor up on the outskirts of Denham Country Park parallel to the river Colne, an ideal spot in open countryside. After tying the ropes tightly around the piling hooks they had placed between the metal corrugated steel lining the sides of the canal, Alice climbed up on the gunwales and put the chimney in place, which had been purposely left off to prevent any damage when going under low bridges. While Alice did this, Sally removed the tiller and pin, then checked inside the engine compartment. Alice went inside the boat, to light the fire. It didn't take long before a good blaze was going. Sally was still on top doing maintenance checks, giving Alice the opportunity to write in private. It didn't take long for her to write down her worry. In large capital letters she wrote one word: alcohol! She folded the paper tightly, then screwed it into a tight ball and without ceremony, she threw it in the fire.

She was still staring at the fire when Sally entered the room.

"Are you alright, Alice?" Sally enquired. Alice was unsure whether or not to tell her what she had done.

After a moment, she said, "I have just taken a very important step towards my recovery." Sally did not press Alice any further on the subject. Instead she enquired if Alice wanted to use the shower first. By the time they had both showered, the boat was warming up nicely. After the meal, Sally produced a pack of playing cards and suggested they have a few games. Sally switched the radio on and they both settled comfortably on the sofa. For Alice, something was missing. She needed a glass in her hand. Remembering how the wine glass of tonic water had helped. She asked Sally to join her in a drink. Sally gave her a sceptical look when Alice returned with two wine glasses.

They clinked glasses and wished each other good health. Sally was most impressed with Alice.

Their first day together as captain and first mate aboard *Poppy*, was going even better than expected. Alice was proving to be a capable boat hand. The remainder of the evening was most enjoyable. Around nine o'clock, Alice went on deck in order to get a better mobile reception as the thick steel of the interior, often interfered with the signal. She rung Mathew and Anne Marie. Then she rang her mum.

They all noticed how much brighter she appeared, which gave them peace of mind. Mathew enquired if mum was being compliant with her medication. Alice reassured him that she was.

Her mum reminded Alice to keep warm and well wrapped up on the boat. This made Alice smile and she told her mum of her memories of the liberty bodice she wore as a child. They both laughed at this. Anne Marie was keen to hear of her mum's health and of the journey so far. All in all, speaking to her family gave her a feeling of contentment. She could feel the love from them. Apparently, Robin had been in contact with all three of them with a message for Alice to make contact. This was on her mind for the rest of the evening. Robin hadn't seemed that interested the last time she made contact. She remembered how he had not returned the sentiments she had given him. However, Alice didn't like the idea of Robin thinking that she wasn't considering him, as that was totally untrue. Now she was feeling a little stronger and thinking more clearly, Alice regretted some of the things she had said to him in the past. She understood that she must also take some responsibility for the situations that had developed over time. By ten o'clock, both Sally and Alice were quite exhausted from the day's travels. Together they had opened and closed many lock gates. Alice had walked miles along the towpath when the distance between the sets of locks had been short as she saw no sense in jumping back on the boat unnecessarily.

Besides, the fresh air and exercise was beginning to put a glow in her sallow complexion and the exercise was helping to strengthen her weak muscles.

Overall, she was regaining her stamina, albeit slowly. The following day, they continued north along the Grand Union Canal, proceeding through the valley of the river Gade, passing by Aspley and Hemel Hempstead, they moored close to bridge 151 for the night. Alice had never visited this area and thought that it might be nice to take a look around the following day. It was less than ten minutes' walk to the town shopping precinct, but Alice preferred the old town's High Street. It was a very enjoyable experience for both of them. They sat for a short while in a pretty tea shop. Alice was content to stare out of the window at the passers-by. She enjoyed watching the young mothers walk by, pushing their prams with such pride. She herself had so much enjoyed the time with her own babies, such precious moments. How lucky she had been to have a family, when so many young couples struggle to conceive. Alice watched elderly people walk by, supporting themselves with sticks, their backs bent and stooping, likely due to osteoporosis, softening and shortening their stature. She had always loved tea shops and had considered, once upon of time, opening one herself. Alice had a large collection of pretty china tea sets at home. She hoped they were safely packed away still. Anne Marie had told her mum of the visit to her home. She told her mum that Robin had packed away her belongings from the rented house, but she didn't tell her mum of the broken table. There had been no need of that information to be passed on. Sally was reading the newspaper and discussing the headlines with Alice. They both shared a common interest in current affairs and were able to have a good debate on how they would put the world to rights. There were many issues they agreed on in terms of educational and health policy. Alice enjoyed these conversations with Sally. Robin and she often debated about such issues, although they had very different opinions.

Alice felt humbled at times, knowing how much effort Sally was putting in to help her. She knew that the greatest gift she could give to Sally was to fully recover and once again make something of her life.

Alice wondered what the driving force was behind Sally, what were her own hopes and aspirations? She knew very little of Sally and up to date she did not appear to want to talk about herself. Following six days of steady sailing north, they reached Northamptonshire. This was familiar territory to Alice. She remembered mooring at Stoke Bruerne in the past. She told Sally it would be an interesting mooring as there is a famous canal museum which was definitely worth a visit. Sally was so pleased to hear the excitement in her friend's voice. The old Alice was emerging from her chrysalis and long may it continue, she thought. The following day waiting for Sally was a whole new experience. Although Alice had been through many tunnels, Blisworth Tunnel was the longest at 3076 yards. It was a very satisfying encounter, especially when they saw the tiny spot of light at the end of the tunnel, getting larger and larger as they approached the exit. Going through the tunnel was also a very wet experience, as the rain water and condensation dripped down on them from the roof. On the exit from the tunnel, something quite extraordinary occurred. Alice began to laugh, softly at first then loudly and boisterously. It was as though she had a life time of laughter trapped inside of her, waiting to burst out. Tears of laughter ran down her hot red face, stinging her from the salty content. Sally was still concentrating on handling the stern of the boat through the tunnel. She was very concerned about her friend who appeared quite hysterical. Eventually, Alice stopped laughing, likely due to exhaustion.

She turned towards Sally and said, "I have been trapped in a tunnel for months with no light at the end, and now I have finally emerged. You see Sally, there is light at the end of the tunnel. I have now seen it for myself and come through."

Somewhat relieved, Sally felt in need of a similar experience herself. Her own thoughts were still consumed with the memories of her son Zak.

These past few weeks helping Alice had blocked out some of the pain, but it was still deep inside her, like a tight knot. Having proved her boating skills and being more than capable of handling the boat, Sally decided to offer the control of the tiller to Alice, allowing herself the opportunity to relax and unwind inside the boat. Sally was feeling the strain of helping Alice and in doing so had neglected her own self-management. Alice was thrilled to know that Sally trusted her with *Poppy*. All alone at the back of the boat, sailing through the picturesque countryside, her hand on the shiny tiller, she could almost feel her mind and body healing. Alice saw a heron standing on the canal bank, patiently looking for a fish to catch. As the boat gently moved forward, the heron took flight and found a new spot on the canal bank. Further along the canal, she witnessed a magnificent pure white swan, gliding majestically through the water. She felt almost surreal. It was as though she was seeing everything for the first time. A veil had been lifted from her non-seeing eyes. Life was looking promising.

Meanwhile, Sally had been hunting through her personal belongings, she eventually found what she was looking for. Her old family albums. As she turned the pages, her heart grew heavy. For most of the album, the photos were of baby Zak, such a healthy baby and a mischievous toddler.

The more pages Sally turned, the more acute her pain. Each school photograph she scrutinised to see if his expression gave anything away. Sally had often wondered if Zak had suffered from low self-esteem, related to the lack of a father figure. Had he felt so different from his peer group? Perhaps when they spoke of activities with their fathers, Zak felt embarrassed, even ashamed. Constantly, Sally tortured herself with endless thoughts of how she could have done things differently. If only, if only! The last few pages of the album were so sad she began to weep. Zak, the sad, troubled looking teenager. No light in his eyes, no life in his body. How gaunt and ill he looked. Her wonderful son, the light of her life. How her heart ached, every fibre of her being was longing for the chance to go back in time and change history, to bring her son back to life, to achieve the impossible. She had lost her son to the evil of street drugs.

She was returned to reality by Alice, who was calling to Sally for a long time. Sally eventually emerged from the inside the boat, looking red eyed and puffy. This did not go unnoticed by Alice. She asked Sally if it was okay for her to take *Poppy* into the lock. Sally nodded her head in agreement. Without looking at Alice, she enquired as to where the windless had been left. Alice pointed to the hatch roof, where the windless was precariously balancing at an uneven angle.

Sally made her way along the gunwales to the stern and when the boat was close enough to the edge of the towpath, she jumped off. Alice hovered around the entrance to the lock while Sally emptied it until the gates creaked, signalling time to push both gates open. Alice drove steadily into the lock and threw Sally the centre rope to keep the boat stable in the double lock, for when the turbulent water rushed in to raise the water level to equal the other side, the hydro power was very strong, requiring great skill to prevent *Poppy* from hitting the interior sides of the lock.

Most of the way, they had shared the double lock with other boaters which halved the workload and side by side the boats were prevented from drifting. Sally slowly opened the paddles, allowing water into the lock chamber. Alice handled the boat well in the lock. Sally hadn't noticed. Her mind was still otherwise preoccupied and remained in that very dark place for the remainder of the day. That evening they moored at bug brook, where they managed to visit the village and pick up fresh supplies of bread, milk and vegetables. It was a very pleasant village with immensely attractive streets. The houses were built from ochre coloured stone giving a rustic appearance. Alice commented on this to Sally, but she either did not appreciated the quaintness and charm of the village, or she was just not interested. Alice could see that Sally was not her usual positive, happy-go-lucky self. Alice sensed that something was amiss. Her first concern was for Sally, but also she wondered if Sally had developed doubts about the journey and helping her. That evening after they had eaten, Alice once again took the time to check out the titles of the books in the book case. She noticed there was a lot on sociology, as expected.

She also noted there were quite a few self-help books and books relating to obsessive and addictive behaviours. One book, different from the rest, caught her attention. It was titled *The Art of Wellbeing*. Alice asked Sally if she could read the book. She agreed and was most pleased that Alice had chosen this particular book, as it was pertinent to her recovery. She hoped that Alice would take on board some of the advice written. Alice read about mindfulness for mental wellbeing and how it allowed a person to become more aware of their stream of thoughts and feelings experienced in order to see how it is possible to become entangled in that stream of thoughts in ways that are not at all helpful. Alice thought about her own experience in the tunnel earlier that day. She had in fact become more aware of that present moment in time and had begun to experience afresh many things around her as if for the first time. Alice asked Sally if she was a great believer in mindfulness. Sally said that reminding yourself to take notice of your thoughts, feelings, body sensations and the world around you is the first step to mindfulness.

Alice was very interested in the subject. It had been a long time since her curiosity had been aroused about a new subject area. She had previously been very passionate about learning.

This was something new and fresh to her. She was eager to learn more. The book outlined formal mindfulness practices, such as yoga and tai-chi. She asked Sally if she had practised this technique and Sally surprised Alice with her frank and honest reply. She told Alice of how she had been trapped inside of herself for years, reliving past problems and negative experiences.

For most of the time she practised mindfulness, but sometimes, the pain broke through and no matter how hard she tried, she could not stop her thoughts taking over. She told Alice that mindfulness means knowing directly what is going on, inside and outside of ourselves, moment by moment.

"And what is going on inside of you, this moment, Sally?" enquired Alice.

Sally wasn't at all surprised that Alice had noticed the pain she was carrying. Her years in nursing had provided her with the necessary observational skills in terms of body language and facial expressions. It was time, thought Sally, time I shared my own pain. They stayed up talking until the early hours of the morning. Sally told Alice about her son Zak. She got out the photograph album that she had been looking at earlier. Sally slowly turned the pages of her life with Zak and in doing so, she cried rivers of tears. This time it was Alice consoling Sally. They cried together as they shared the rich tapestry of their lives, the good and the bad. Sally told Alice that although she had practised mindfulness, she felt at times it was akin to self- compassion, which she felt was conflicting for her as she was so furious at herself for being depressed. Sally told Alice the fury within herself was poisoning her thoughts and creating resentments and self-loathing. However, with time, the conflict had eased or at least become manageable for most of the time. She told Alice that true self-compassion means accepting who you are, your own light and darkness and forgiving yourself for all of it. By the time they went to bed, weary and red eyed, they both knew a lot more about each other. They slept in late the following day, both of them looking the worse for wear and puffy eyed, but also something else.

They felt cleansed. Sharing their innermost thoughts and feelings it had been cathartic for them. It was afternoon before they managed to untie the boat and make headway towards their next destination. They had been travelling for three hours when the sky became overcast and storm clouds were gathering. A cold north wind was blowing fiercely, driving the boat across the cut into shallow water. The boat did not respond well in shallow water, adding to the slow response of the propeller. They were well aware of the urgent need to moor the boat before the storm was directly overhead and the heavens opened. They were way out in the countryside, far from even the smallest village or hamlet when Sally noticed two narrow boats moored in the distance. Thinking it must be a safe spot to stay, they made their way towards the boats, intending to stay for a while until the storm settled.

As they got closer, it became obvious that the boats were in very poor condition and it was likely they had not been moved for some time. Weeds were growing out of the fenders, the boat paintwork had green algae and moss engrained in and the windows were thick with dust and mud. The curtains were tattered and torn and on the roof of the boats was enough rubbish to fill two skips.

Then the rain began to fall, soft at first, soon changing into a torrential downpour. Now they had no choice but to stop. Sally pulled the boat alongside the towpath. The wind was blowing fiercely and as Alice jumped off the boat she didn't land quite right, slipped on the muddy towpath and she banged her head against the corrugated metal lining of the canal bank. Sally quickly switched the engine over to neutral, grabbed the back rope and jumped to the towpath. She called for help, hoping that someone just may be in one of the derelict looking boats. Sally was struggling to hold the boat against the wind. She really needed to grab the centre rope to pull the boat in alongside. The back of the boat was drifting out to the centre of the canal. Alice was very dazed from the knock to her head and she had blood pouring from a head wound. The blood was running down her muddy face and the rain was making the towpath worse by the minute. She crawled along the towpath towards Sally, just as there was some movement from the boat next to *Poppy*. Somehow, Alice pulled herself to an upright position by pulling herself up on the taught rope as Sally was struggling with the boat.

The added pressure on the rope was a heavy strain for Sally. She had no gloves on to protect her and the course fibres of the rope were tearing into her flesh. A thin and gaunt looking young man very slowly staggered towards them. He never spoke a single word, not even a grunt. He took the rope off Sally and motioned for her to climb on the gunwales and retrieve the centre rope. Sally had no other choice.

The wind speed was increasing and the rain continued to pour in torrents. She struggled against the elements and managed to retrieve the rope. With every ounce of strength she possessed, Sally pulled on the centre rope until eventually the length of the boat was parallel with the bank. She called to Alice to get the mooring chains that were hung in the front cratch. Still feeling dazed and uncoordinated, Alice retrieved the rings. She placed one set in the gap between the corrugated steel at the stern and the other at the bow. The young man was still holding onto the front ropes for dear life. His thin legs looked like they might snap under the strain. Sally tied the back rope and approached the young man who had most definitely helped to prevent a potential dangerous situation. With everything happening so quickly, Sally didn't have time to pay too much attention to their saviour, but now as she coaxed him to give her the rope. She was horrified to see how ill he looked and how unkempt his appearance was. He looked to be about twenty-five years old, but it was hard to put an age on him. His hair was long and dark. It was matted together as though it had never seen a comb, never mind a wash. He was sallow looking and unshaven. His eyes though, that was what haunted her the most. Those eyes, that look. It was a mirror image of Zak. She gasped with horror as he passed her the rope. His bare arms were covered with injection site sores and abscesses. Sally took a deep breath and swallowed hard. She offered her hand to him as she thanked him for his help and kindness. He looked right through her; never said a word and walked back to his boat, the wind and rain further torturing his damaged young body.

Meanwhile, Alice had observed exactly the same and was equally disturbed. She was also ashamed of herself for coming so close to ruining her own life just as surely this young man had done. The tragedy of it all seemed so unjust and she wondered, not for the first time, how hard life is for some and not others. With Sally's help she managed to climb back on the boat. They were both very wet and cold.

The fire was not yet lit and the chimney needed to be put on. Alice was in no fit state to do anything except to lay down. The blood was gushing from her head wound. So it was left to Sally to continue with the chores. Her hands were cold, wet and sore from the ropes. The mud had gotten into the wounds on her hands. She was at risk of infection getting inside the cuts, but she went outside and put the chimney in position. Then, without taking off her sodden clothes, she went back inside to light the fire. Alice was shivering uncontrollably on the sofa. Her face was a mess. Having taken off her own wet clothes, she put on the nearest thing, which was a towelled bathrobe. She gathered some towels and a face cloth and proceeded to help Alice out of her wet, blood stained clothes. Sally wrapped the towels around Alice and gently wiped the mud off of her face with the wet facecloth, revealing a deep jagged laceration below her left ear extending to just above the chin line. The wound could wait. She needed to give Alice a hot drink. Her teeth were chattering and she could not keep a limb still. The quickest and most substantial drink on board was a soup in a cup. Sally handed this to Alice who wrapped her hands around the mug and sipped the soup. The fire was beginning to warm the boat through and the colour was returning to both of their faces. While Alice sipped the drink, Sally had a warm shower. As she felt the deliciously warm water cascade over her, Sally began to weep. The adrenaline high which had kept her going throughout the ordeal had enabled her to deal with a difficult situation, but now that the adrenaline was returning to near normal levels her body was feeling the aftershock. Her mind began to wander as she relived the moment, when she truly looked at the young man who had helped them. The look in his eyes was haunting her. She felt compelled to show him compassion and to express how grateful they both were for his assistance. She decided the best reward was not money, but food, good, substantial food. She scrubbed the ingrained mud from her hands, causing her much discomfort.

Sally then bathed her wounds with antiseptic and covered the worst of them with dressings. Sally dressed herself warmly in jeans and a heavy knit sweater. She called out to Alice and encouraged her to have a shower. Like a dutiful child, Alice followed her instructions. The shower calmed her down and gradually, the shaking stopped. Alice wrapped herself in a bath sheet to keep herself warm. She rested on the only available area in the small bathroom, the toilet seat. There she sat rocking and hugging herself for a good ten minutes. Meanwhile, Sally was in the galley preparing food. She knew how important it was for her to pull herself together.

Instinctively, Alice realised that at this moment in time, her friend needed her more than ever before. After seeing the young man who most likely reminded her of Zak, Sally was likely traumatised herself and the whole fiasco with *Poppy*, which was her home, would have reinforced her pain. Alice wiped the steam from the bathroom mirror and checked the wound on her face. It was still bleeding profusely. She knew that the hot shower had increased the blood flow, and indirectly that was a good process, for it helped to cleanse the wound of any bacteria that may have entered subcutaneously. She found the first aid box in the bathroom cupboard, it was surprisingly well stocked. Alice cleansed the wound with a normal saline soaked gauze swab then cut small strips of dressing tape to make small skin closures across the wound, bringing the wound edges together. She then applied an iodine soaked gauze dressing across the wound and secured it in place with an adhesive outer dressing. Alice once again checked out her reflection. She looked as though she had come from a war zone, her wet hair hanging around her tired looking face. She tied her hair back and dressed in jeans and fleece top. When Alice entered the galley she wasn't sure what words of comfort she could offer her friend, instead Alice offered her help in the kitchen, hoping for an opportunity to offer some soothing words.

Sally nodded and passed Alice a potato peeler and a large bag of potatoes. To Alice's astonishment she asked her to peel the lot. Meanwhile, Sally retrieved four medium sized tinfoil casserole dishes from the cupboard. Between them, they made four very wholesome cottage pies. Alice guessed who the other three were for. Sure enough, once the pies were ready, Sally wrapped each one in tinfoil and wrapped a clean tea towel around each one. She asked Alice if she felt well enough to help her carry the food next door to the young man's boat. Alice said of course she would help.

Alice realised that this was Sally's way of coping with the trauma. The rain had stopped and the wind was no more than a light breeze as they stepped off the boat. The tow path was terribly muddy as they slipped and slid the short distance to the boat as they made their way with their offerings of gratitude. Close up, the boat was even worse than expected. Sally knocked loudly on the window on the towpath side to inform the occupant that they were stepping on board.

They knocked loudly on the cabin door. A dog was barking and whining inside the boat. They looked at one another. This may not be a safe situation for two vulnerable women. They had no idea how many other people were on board or if the dog was dangerous. Eventually, the door was slightly opened, then a little bit more until once again they came face to face with the unfortunate young man. There was deep sorrow in his soulful eyes. It ripped Alice's heart in two.

She thought of her own two healthy children and four healthy step children. How had this young man come into such a sad and desolate situation. Where was his family and friends? How come society had let him down so badly? Although she did not realise this at that precise moment, this vision was to remain in her mind forever; this ultimately was her calling. Without speaking, Sally passed him the first dish of food. His haunted look, lifted a little and by the third dish his face was transformed. He gave them a crooked smile and nodded his head. No words were spoken.

He knew they were showing kindness and gratitude, it was the first time in many months that anyone had been kind to him. He placed one dish on the floor of the boat, unwrapped it and whistled his dog. The dog ran to the dish, wagging its tail and eagerly ate the food. He gently closed the door on them, signalling an end to the encounter. It wasn't the end, though, for Sally and Alice. The whole episode would have a long lasting effect. For Sally, it began that very same evening. The moment she fell asleep, her dreams turned into nightmares. She relived every painful moment with Zak. Sometimes his face was the face of the young man in the next boat. Somehow, all of the love, the pain and the all-consuming feeling that she had let him down had crept into her dreams. His beautiful face and those sad brown eyes. Zak's face and the young man's, morphed into one. They were the same person, except one was alive. But for how long was anyone's guess. Alice also had a restless night. She allowed herself to wallow in her own painful memories. Subconsciously, she tried very hard to only remember the good times and extinguish the bad feelings. Sally had taught her that the only way forward was to let go of the past, and only then would healing begin to take place.

CHAPTER ELEVEN

The next day they continued their journey along the Grand Union Canal, sharing the work load. When Alice became tired after working the heavy lock gates, Sally took over the task and allowed Alice to steer *Poppy* into the lock chambers. At Norton Junction, where the Leicester section of the Grand Union network diverged with the main London-Birmingham line, they once again moored the boat as their provisions were getting low. This gave them the opportunity for some well-deserved respite and time to eat a late lunch. The fresh air and exercise was gradually putting the flesh back on Alice's bones, her complexion was improving and her hair condition was somewhat better. The psychological trauma of the previous day was still fresh in both of their minds, although neither of them spoke about the event for fear of returning to the pain and reinforcing the emotions of the whole episode. Once more travelling along the canal, they enjoyed the peace and quiet, it was so tranquil, almost as though they were living an alternate existence in a different period of time, Alice thought. Her reverie was not to last, as the canal was gradually winding towards civilization, when the canal was in close proximity to the M1 motorway. They followed this route for two miles and it reminded them both of the fast paced life away from the inland waterways. They continued west at Norton

Junction, passing through the Braunston Summit, three hundred and fifty-seven feet of partially subterranean landscape. They travelled through the Braunston Tunnel, the seventh longest that is currently navigable. This time Alice steered *Poppy* into the dark and gloomy underworld of the waterways, allowing Sally the opportunity to emerge from her own pseudo tunnel of life as she herself had experienced.

However this time there was no hysterical laughter, just smiles all round.

The following days they fell into a steady, regular pattern, travelling between five and seven hours a day, depending on the weather conditions. Some evenings they watched the television, providing the aerial was able to pick up a decent signal. Otherwise they listened to the radio or read quietly. Alice had always enjoyed reading and was content to relax for hours with a good book. She was learning so much from the extensive range of psychology and sociology books.

Of particular interest and value to Alice was the self-help books. Sally recommended she read *The Road Less Travelled* by M Scott Peck and *Feeling Good: The New Mood Therapy* by Dr David Burns. Although at first sceptical, Alice was totally hooked. What resonated most was his evaluation that "it is only your beliefs about yourself that can affect the way you feel. Others can say or think whatever they want about you, but only your thoughts will influence your emotions." Reading this helped Alice to feel empowered, she began to realize and understand more about herself and how she was responsible for her own self-healing.

Their friendship deepened, it was as though they had been drawn inexorably together. They laid their lives bare to scrutiny from one another. Sometimes returning to the pain and reliving it. Talking to each other and rationalising their thoughts, reinforced the healing process equally.

They were close to the journey's end, approaching Birmingham. Alice had moored there many times before with Robin. She particularly enjoyed the Gas Street Basin moorings, with their lively cosmopolitan feel. She told Sally of the many shops, bars and restaurants. They had purposely avoided areas of pubs and bars with the best intentions and now Alice would come face to face with this type of scene, where young and old would be socialising and having fun. Sally was concerned.

She felt very proud of Alice and how well she was managing. Sally also realised that she had not been faced with temptation either and this could now be the biggest hurdle Alice was to face so far. Alice of course, was also aware of the possible temptations that lay ahead. She was sensible enough to realize this was inevitable and she concentrated on drawing strength from the advice in the many self-help books that she had read and, word for word, committed to her memory. Alice was thinking only positive thoughts. She liked the idea of dressing up and going to a nice restaurant for a meal. Plans beyond Birmingham had never been discussed. Alice felt that it was time to approach the subject. With trepidation she enquired about the return journey to London. Sally had been wondering when Alice would bring up the subject. She shook her head and to Alice's surprise, told her that the plans she had put in place were as yet uncertain.

Alice did not want to pry further even though her own future was uncertain. She felt somewhat adrift and a little confused, although she trusted Sally implicitly and decided to put the worry on hold. After securing the boat on a mooring in Gas Street Basin, they decided to explore the surrounding area. Sally was most impressed with this new territory. It was the farthest she had travelled from

London and she was not disappointed. They crossed over the bridge, following the signs for the town centre. As they were crossing the bridge, Sally's mobile phone rang. Alice could not help but listen in on the conversation. It was rare for Sally to receive a call and she was intrigued, especially when she heard Sally mention Nottingham Castle Marina. The conversation ended and Sally smiled at Alice.

"I think we need to sit down and talk," she said.

They walked a short distance, admiring the many bars and restaurants, trying to decide which one to visit. Alice's attention was drawn to the French restaurant, Café Rouge. She loved French cuisine and suggested to Sally this might be a good choice. The restaurant was close to the water front and very pleasant.

They ordered warm camembert cheese and fresh bread to share with mixed olives on the side, followed by fresh green salad and chicken. Sitting compatibly together, Sally took Alice's hands in hers. She began by apologising to Alice for not confiding in her sooner about her plans. She explained that, until now, nothing had been set in stone, only preliminary plans had been arranged. Sally went on to explain that she had a very good friend who was currently renting a flat in Nottingham close to the university, where she worked as a psychology lecturer.

Her friend's name was Angela and they had hoped to meet in Birmingham. However, Angela, for a number of reasons was unable to make it. She had suggested that they travel onwards to Nottingham where she would meet up with them and help Sally with the return journey to London. Alice gasped, she felt worried. Nottingham was rather close to home, and she wasn't quite ready to face that hurdle yet. Sally saw the worried look on her friend's face.

"That's not all, Alice," she softly said. "Angela works at the university. She has been looking into a number of post-graduate programs for you to apply for. Amongst them is a post graduate diploma in Drug and Alcohol Rehabilitation. How do you feel about returning to study? With your back ground in nursing and a science degree, you are an ideal candidate." Alice was speechless. For a moment, she said nothing while she turned over the possibilities in her mind. She knew the university well, having spent some time there doing her degree. She fondly remembered Cripps Hall and the amazing lecture theatres. She had spent many happy hours on the university campus. Just thinking about it created a warm glow of memories long gone. Sally interrupted her thoughts.

"Think about it, Alice, it is only one option, there are others. You have the Aptitude, the skills and first-hand experience, with so much to offer in terms of your compassion." Alice nodded her head.

"I will certainly give it a great deal of thought," she answered.

They sat a while after finishing their food, drinking coffee and talking through the next stage of the journey from Birmingham to Nottingham. They planned to stay one more day in Birmingham as they had a forty-eight hour mooring spot and Sally had never visited the area before and there was lots she wanted to see. They walked along the towpath in silence, Alice mulling over the idea of going back to university and Sally thinking about the long journey back down the Grand Union Canal to London. Angela had no experience of boating, unlike Alice who had been remarkably helpful running the boat. Her boating skills were quite something; her experience shone through. The following morning, Alice was up bright and early, with a spring in her step and a huge grin on her face. She made tea and took a mug into Sally who was still snuggled up in bed and enjoying a day off. She accepted the tea gratefully and even in her sleepy, half-awake frame of mind, Sally knew that she was seeing a glimpse of the old Alice.

While sat up in bed, sipping her tea, she could have sworn that she heard Alice singing. Quietly at first, then much more emphatic. By the time Sally was up and dressed, the breakfast table was set with all of the trimmings. Eggs were boiling in the pan and the delicious smell of toast was drifting through the boat. She could not believe her eyes. Alice looked vibrant. Her expression was so alive, almost as though someone had switched a light on in Alice's mind, where until recently it had been on dim. Her whole demeanour was of a woman with confidence, passion and drive.

"Good morning Alice," said Sally, without taking her eyes of her. "I must say, you look extremely well today." Alice smiled kindly at Sally.

"I have done a lot of soul searching since last night. I have so much to thank you for, there is no way I can ever repay you for the kindness you have shown. Except one way. To take your advice and make a success of my life, to take back control and help others."

"Wow, that was very prolific," said Sally. "Does that mean you will seriously consider applying for the course?"

"Without a single doubt, I am making a commitment to you today. A promise that I have every intention of keeping." In another life, Alice would have clinked glasses and made a toast with wine. She would have celebrated until the early hours of the morning. But not this Alice. She had been through the worst of it and although her demons were fading like an unwelcome mist, they still loitered in the background, waiting to weave back in, catching her when not aware. Alice had every intention of being on her guard, day and night, for the remainder of her life. She had a goal. A realistic goal, that was achievable.

All thanks to Sally and to Angela, who she had yet to meet. She was so excited and eager to be on her way to a new future, but first Alice needed some suitable clothes for possibly a very important interview and she wanted to be well prepared for the occasion. Currently, none of her clothes fit her properly, despite having gained a few pounds in weight. Sally decided not to go shopping with Alice, explaining that it wasn't really her thing, she preferred to relax with a good book and recharge her batteries for the journey to Nottingham. "After all, Alice. I also have a long return journey to London ahead of me, so I am going to make the most of this opportunity. Perhaps later we can explore the city together." Of course Alice did not mind, she completely understood. She wasn't fond of shopping either, but this was important. She made her way to the Bull Ring Centre where she hoped to find what she needed. It didn't take her long to realise that perhaps looking in charity shops might be a better idea. Having checked out a couple of shops without success, Alice called into a café for a cup of tea. While waiting for the waitress to bring the drink over, she used the time to ring her family to tell them of her good news. Her family were still not aware of the full extent of her illness. However, they had surmised that she was likely to be suffering from depression, but out of displaced kindness never raised the subject.

Mathew and Anne Marie were delighted to hear of their mum's plans to once again return to the university.

They enquired about her planned living arrangements and financial security. Although not sure herself, she told them that she hoped to get part time work at the hospital and also to apply for supply work that would fit around her studies. Specifically, she hoped to work weekend shifts.

They appeared to be satisfied with her reply. Her mum however, had other ideas. She suggested that Alice should move back to her lovely home and commute daily to the university. Her mum's main concern was that her daughter's money was still invested in the house where Robin and his family were currently living. Alice laughed when her mum said that it was luxurious living. "Oh Mum, its only bricks and mortar at the end of the day, and you and I both know that I couldn't possibly move back in. The only hope for Robin and I is a fresh start, that is what I am hoping for." Apparently, Robin had been to visit her mum a number of times and was always kind and polite with her. She said he always looked sad and despondent, although they very rarely discussed Alice, for fear of opening a can of worms. Finally, Alice reassured her mum, after explaining her plans to find work at the hospital. The waitress came with the tea and Alice sent her love and good wishes. She is on her way home, thought her mum, my daughter is coming home. Back on the charity shop trail, it proved to be more successful after the short break. She found a well-fitting pencil skirt and box jacket. She purchased a white shirt style blouse and a pair of navy court shoes. They all fitted perfectly.

CHAPTER TWELVE

The following day they set off on their journey from Gas Street Basin to the centre of Nottingham. Eager to get there, some days they sailed eight hours or more. Every day was a day closer to Alice's destiny; a future that she was determined to make a success of. In the evenings she read until she could no longer keep her eyes open. Sally had kindly chosen a number of suitable books for her to read in preparation for her planned course at the University of Nottingham. Alice had really set her mind to it now, with a burning passion. It had been a lot of years since her degree and she needed to be in the right mind-set for study. Alice realized how different the course material would be presented, and the teaching methods too. In addition, it was likely she would need to present her work in the form of a word document, not a hard copy that was accepted in the past. Once in Nottingham, Alice hoped to be busy one way or another, all of which would help to distract her and continue with her own healing.

They moored close to Castle Marina, not too far from the city centre, but close enough for Angela to have a steady walk along the towpath to meet them. Alice felt a little shy of meeting her, although she already knew so much about her from Sally who had reminisced most evenings with Alice. She was aware of how they had met as young students and how they had immediately felt at ease with each other. Alice laughed with Sally when she re-encountered some of the amusing antics they got up to at university. She guessed that it was likely that Sally had filled Angela in on her background. She didn't mind this at all. Better to be honest and it was far easier with strangers than family. Alice still believed that there was no need to tell her own family and certainly not Robin about the extent of her troubles. It wasn't that she was worried about him judging her, the truth was that she still felt ashamed and embarrassed. Sally suggested that they walk along the towpath and meet Angela as she made her way towards *Poppy*. Of course Sally was not familiar with the area, but Alice, well, she felt almost at home.

Everything was familiar as they strolled along the well-kept path. She had walked along this stretch many times before with Robin. They often sailed into Nottingham to meet friends in the town for an evening out. It was an achievable distance for them to travel from where their own boat was moored. Alice was tempted to suggest that they sail *Poppy* towards the marina and show her the boat. She didn't have a key but the marina office had a spare. Having given this much thought, Alice decided against this in case Robin was visiting the boat. As they walked compatibly together, Alice told Sally about the Theatre Royal and suggested they might watch a show together before returning to London. Sally rather liked the idea and planned to discuss it with Angela.

Alice needn't have worried about meeting Angela, for she was as warm and friendly as Sally. She was amusing too, and full of joy. She radiated happiness, creating a very light hearted ambience. They returned to the boat and sat around the drop leaf table together.

Sally had left the table prepared with a light afternoon tea. She made a pot of tea and joined Angela and Alice. Although they had a lot of catching up to do, both Angela and Sally made Alice the focus of their attentions. Angela, reached into her very large handbag and produced a Manilla envelope. Passing it to Alice she smiled and told her that it was a passport to a new life.

She then reached back into her handbag, rummaged around for a few seconds and produced a bunch of keys. Passing them to Alice, she said, "I desperately need someone responsible to look after my flat while I am away. You will be doing me a great favour if you agree? It is close to the university and within very easy reach of the town centre. Please say yes," smiled Angela. "Oh and one more favour, are you okay with cats? I have the sweetest little kitten who is really going to miss me, his name is Charlie."

Alice felt truly blessed, she could not believe what she was hearing. These two wonderful ladies whom she had only recently met were surely angels in disguise… A flat and a fluffy companion was a dream come true. What had Alice done to deserve such good fortune?

"I will be utterly delighted, it is a big fat yes from me," grinned Alice.

"Then you had better start packing!" smiled Sally, "and whatever you do, don't forget to pack your interview outfit, I guess you look pretty amazing in it?"

"We will take you to the flat and introduce you to Charlie, then I can collect my luggage for my adventure down the Grand Union Canal to London," laughed Angela.

Alice left the two friends to chat while she scurried around the boat, collecting her possessions.

Sally gave her two psychology books to pack along with her other items. Then she passed Alice a gift wrapped parcel.

"For you to open, once settled," said Sally. Together they walked into the city centre. Alice pointed out the theatre and suggested they check out if there were any available tickets for the next performance. Sadly, the lady in the box office informed them that the show was a sell-out. Disappointed, they made a pact to one day, in the not too distant future, meet up and catch a show. The flat was as described, indeed a short distance from the centre. As they approached, Alice felt butterflies in her tummy and a sensation of freedom such as she had never felt before. It was as though she had been in a prison of her own making. The very moment Alice stepped foot through the door, she knew that this was a new beginning for her.

No longer would she be the victim. This time she would be the heroine of her own story.